OTHER BOOKS by KASSANDRA LAMB

THE CALL OF THE WOOF

A Marcia Banks and Buddy Mystery

Kassandra Lamb

author of the Kate Huntington Mysteries

The Call of the Woof
A Marcia Banks and Buddy Mystery

Published in the United States of America by *misterio press*,
a Florida limited liability company
http://misteriopress.com

~~~~~~~~~~~~

Edited by Marcy Kennedy

Cover and interior design by Melinda VanLone, Book Cover Corner

Photo credits: silhouette of woman and dog by Majivecka
(right of use purchased from dreamstime.com)

ISBN 13: 978-0-9974674-5-1 (misterio press LLC)
ISBN 10: 0-9974674-5-2

To all those who have suffered from traumatic brain injury.
I can only imagine your struggles.

CHAPTER ONE

I had a dizzying moment of *déjà vu* when Jake Black called.

"Marcia, I need you to take Felix."

"Wha'?" Okay, so I'm not a brilliant conversationalist when dragged out of a sound sleep at three-thirty in the morning.

"I need you to get Felix for me. They've got him at Buckland County Animal Services."

"Huh? Why?"

"Janey and I have been arrested."

"For what?"

"For robbery."

"Tell me you've called a lawyer," I said, now fully awake. The last time a client of mine had been incarcerated, he'd used his one phone call to call *me*, instead of an attorney.

"Yeah, Janey's using her call for that. But I'm not at all sure what animal services will do with Felix. I don't know that they'll realize he's a valuable service dog."

Adrenaline shot through my system. Surely the public shelter wouldn't destroy or adopt out an animal belonging to someone who was only accused of a crime, not convicted yet. But I understood Jake's concern. Mix-ups happened.

My feet hit the floor with a thud. "Okay, I'll get over there first thing in the morning."

Jake blew out a sigh. "Thanks." He told me where to find the keys to their house, hidden in a fake rock, and gave me the security system code.

"'I know it's a lot to ask," he said, "but you could stay at the house? I mean live there, you don't have to stay all the time. For a day or two, until we get this straightened out."

"Actually that solves a problem I have. I could use a place to stay for a few days. Keep me posted."

I sat on the edge of the bed, in the tee-shirt I'd swiped from Will to use as a nightshirt, and tried to wrap my brain around the Blacks being arrested for robbery.

Jake Black had regaled me last year with stories of his mis-spent youth when I'd trained with him and Felix. But he was now in his forties, a business owner, combat veteran, husband of twenty-some years, father of a college-aged daughter.

And his wife? Janey Black was a sweetheart, the type of person who'd drive back to the grocery store if a cashier gave her too much change.

I shook my head.

It was unlikely I'd get back to sleep at this point, so I threw on capris and a loose-fitting tropical shirt. I ran a comb through my hair—I was retraining myself to think of it as auburn rather than brunette, now that the Florida sun had blessed me with red highlights. Pulling the long strands up into a ponytail, I stared at the circles under my eyes. They were almost as dark as the brown irises.

Still I opted to forego makeup. I had a dozen things to do before I could make good on my promise to get Felix.

Today, my Black Lab-Rottie mix, Buddy and I were moving out of our house temporarily, while an exterminator fumigated it for termites and then a contractor repaired the damage the little buggers had done.

Now, if you live in the Northeast you might be thinking, *Fumigate? For termites?*

But these are not your standard, run-of-the-mill termites. Florida always likes to be bigger and better in the bug department, with flying two-inch palmetto bugs instead of roaches and drywood termites in addition to the regular kind.

The latter had gotten into the rafters of my cement-block cottage and my roof was about to fall in.

I'd packed up some things that might be damaged by the fumigation process, and a neighbor had offered to store the boxes for me. But I still needed to gather my clothes and some belongings Buddy and I would need for the next few days.

At a little after six, I carried the first of my storage boxes next door. Edna Mayfair and her nephew were early birds. I knew they'd be up.

I knocked on the frame of the screen door. The inside door hung open to catch the slight morning breeze. The cottage didn't have central air.

September might mean cooler temperatures for most of the country, but not in central Florida. Down here, it's still relentlessly in the nineties with high humidity day after day, until at least mid-October.

"Come on in," Edna called out from somewhere in the recesses of the house.

I stepped into the front room of the shotgun cottage she was renting. It smelled faintly of mildew and dogs. I walked on through to the kitchen, where I found her and Dexter already poring over the plans for their new motel while munching on their breakfast cereal.

Dexter, barefoot in cutoffs and a tee-shirt, jumped up to take the box from me. "I'll put it in the spare room."

He was about my age—early thirties—but I tended to think of him as younger, probably because he was a brick or two short of a load. But he was a sweet guy, always eager to help.

"Marcia, help us out here," his great aunt said from her lawn chair next to a wobbly card table.

Guilt tightened my chest. I hated that Edna, in her eighties, had lost everything she owned and had to start over, because I'd attracted a crazy person to our little town of Mayfair—a crazy person who'd burned down her motel.

But Edna didn't seem to hold it against me. She was moving

forward with what bordered on glee.

She stabbed a finger at the drawing on the table. "We can't decide between Gothic columns for the porch, or a more Victorian look."

I glanced over her shoulder at the artist's rendition of the new motel, and decided I could stop feeling guilty. The building depicted in the drawing was a lot bigger and nicer than the one that had burned down.

"The Gothic ones are classier," I said.

Of course, any guest who took one look at Edna would realize "classy" was the wrong adjective. As usual, her gray hair stuck out in all directions and today's muumuu displayed a chaotic array of brightly colored hibiscus blooms.

I gave a slight shake of my head. "But Victorian would probably fit the small-town ambiance better. Where are Bennie and Bo?"

"Out back. Go on out and say hi."

My mind brought up an image of the derelict property's backyard—a tangle of palmettos, wild flowers and weeds that would require a machete to get through it. Besides, saying hello to her rambunctious Springer Spaniels would take up precious time. They would both demand a thorough ear scratch.

"I'd better not. I've got to get going. Hey Dexter, can you help me with the rest of the boxes?"

He did, and we stowed them in one of the two bedrooms that some previous owner had tacked onto the back of the original master bedroom. It was blessedly cool compared to the front part of the house.

"Don't worry, Marcia. We keep the window shakers on all the time back here." Dexter gestured toward an air conditioner rattling away in the main bedroom's window. "You won't get any mold in your things."

That was a relief. Mold was a constant threat in humid Florida.

Buddy and I made it to Buckland County Animal Services

Center as they were opening. The young woman who greeted me couldn't have been nicer. "We've kept Felix quarantined, considering how valuable he is."

I quietly let out a sigh. Not everybody understood what went into training a true service dog. You didn't just give them some obedience lessons and slap a vest on them. It took six months of intensive work to train them, and the not-for-profit agency I trained for charged ten thousand dollars for each dog, which didn't even cover all the costs. The rest were made up with grants and donations.

There was a little bit of discussion with the young woman about whether she could legally release Felix to me. I'd brought my copy of his training certificate, but I didn't have anything in writing from Jake.

Felix's frenzied greeting of me helped cinch the deal. When he saw me, his naturally mournful-looking eyes lit up and his whole rear end wiggled, not just his stubby tail. He scrambled across the tiled floor, his nails clattering and scraping.

"Well, he certainly knows you," the woman said with a chuckle.

I crouched and hugged Felix, then gave him my signal for down—a hand parallel to the floor moving down a few inches. He immediately plopped down on his belly.

Buddy assumed the signal included him and he lay down beside the brindle boxer-and-something-a-lot-bigger mix. I'm not a huge fan of brindle, but Felix's coat has a lot of gold mixed in with the darker shades of black and tan. On him, brindle looks good.

I smiled at the animal control lady. "You can call the jail if you like and see if they'll let you talk to his owner."

She shrugged. "I guess that isn't necessary."

She led me over to a counter and handed me some paperwork to sign. Always, there is paperwork. "What all's involved in learning to do what you do?" she asked.

I looked up from the papers into her smooth twenty-something face, framed by frizzy brown curls. Her fresh eagerness made me feel old, even though I'd probably only been on the planet a half dozen years longer than she had.

"You mean train dogs?"

She nodded. "Service dogs for injured veterans, like you do."

"We mostly work with vets with PTSD and other psychological issues, but some of them have physical injuries too." I quickly scanned the pages in front of me and signed. I handed the papers back to her. "Each organization does things their own way. For the agency I'm with, you train under another trainer, usually the director, Mattie—Mathilda Jones." I dug one of Mattie's cards out of my purse. "Give her a call. There's far more need for trained dogs than there are trainers to produce them. You'd be doing important work."

The woman grinned and took the card from me. "Thanks. Can I tell her we talked, uh…," she glanced at my name that I'd printed on the papers, "Ms. Banks?"

"Sure." I gave her a big smile, snapped the leash I'd brought on Felix's collar, and the dogs and I headed for the Blacks' home.

I'd been there before, during the final stages of Felix and Jake's training as partners, but I'd forgotten how big it was. The sprawling rancher, on an acre of carefully landscaped lawn in a neighborhood of equally large houses, proclaimed that its owners were upper middle class—in income at least, despite the fact that they acted like "plain folks," as my mom would say.

I'd just retrieved a set of two keys from the fake rock when I thought I saw movement out of the corner of my eye. I glanced over to the freestanding three-car garage that housed the Blacks' motorcycles and Jake's workshop. It baked in the mid-morning sun, nothing more than little lizards scuttling around it.

I jogged in that direction, the dogs on my heels. The house could fall into a sinkhole and Jake might not even notice, but if anything happened to his garage and the bikes inside, he'd go ballistic.

A shadow wavered across the huge white door.

I jerked around and saw a pants leg as someone climbed into an oversized white pickup parked on the street.

Air rushed out of my lungs. That's what I'd seen in my peripheral vision, a shadow of someone walking to their vehicle, projected against the garage by the slanting sun.

Nonetheless I made a circuit around its perimeter, again the dogs acting as the rear guard. Everything was locked up tight.

I was about to turn back toward the house when Felix started sniffing around the side door of the garage. I walked over.

Crapola!

That sure looked like fresh scratch marks around the deadbolt. Had someone tried to pick the lock? Worse yet, had someone actually gotten inside?

I turned back toward the street, but the white truck was gone.

CHAPTER TWO

Inside, I found Felix's bowls in the kitchen and freshened his water, then poured some in Buddy's travel bowl and put it on the floor nearby.

A key rack, in the shape of an Army helmet, caught my eye by the kitchen door. The keys were labeled but there wasn't one marked *garage*. I opened drawers until I found the inevitable junk drawer. Rooting through it, I discovered several random keys.

Leaving the dogs to lap up some water, I went outside with those keys. The second one fit the side door's lock.

The garage was the neatest one I'd ever seen. On one side was a workshop area. Three motorcycles were parked on the other side, one with three wheels rather than two—like a giant tricycle.

Jake's sidecar, where Felix rode, sat along one wall. Nothing seemed amiss, so I locked up and headed back toward the house.

A weird feeling crept up my neck, a sense of being watched. I spun around. But the driveway was empty, as was the section of the street that I could see from here. A slight breeze rustled in the line of trees that separated the driveway from the neighbor's property.

I shrugged off the creepy feeling and went inside.

By the time I'd called the motel in nearby Ormond-By-The-Sea and delayed my reservation for a day, I'd decided that I was overreacting to a few scratches, a shadow and someone innocently climbing into a vehicle.

After all, white pickup trucks were a dime a dozen in Florida.

If I remembered correctly, Jake even had one.

Leaning my butt against the edge of the kitchen counter, I smiled to myself at the motherism—*a dime a dozen*. Then the smile grew wider as I realized I no longer reacted negatively when I thought or said some old-fashioned phrase picked up from my mother. My unusual name—pronounced Mar-see-a rather than Marsha—along with my prim and proper speech patterns, had gotten me teased a good bit as a kid, but I was working on that, along with some other things, with my counselor.

Unfortunately, I'd had to suspend my counseling sessions for a couple of months due to finances. Not only were the fumigation and repairs costing me a bundle, but I'd had to forego starting with a new dog once Jenny, my latest trainee, was placed with her new owner. Living in a motel room was not conducive to the early stages of training a service dog.

At least I'm saving some bucks by staying here for a day or two.

I went out into the spacious living room and crossed it to the hallway leading to my home away from home, the guest suite the Blacks had originally set up for their daughter, to give her some additional privacy in her teens. She was away at college now.

I'd known it was there—the hallway had been pointed out when I'd been here last year for training sessions—but I'd never been in it. I threw open the door and stopped cold.

It was palatial. A big sunken living room stretched out in front of me, with an oversized sliding glass door that looked out on the property's large lanai and a backyard full of lush foliage. Across from me was a closed door, the bedroom I assumed.

I glanced down at the dogs who'd followed me. "Pretty impressive, isn't it?"

Felix seemed blasé, which made sense since he lived with this bounty regularly. Buddy looked up at me and gave a small wag of his tail.

"Aw, all you two care about is where the treats are stashed."

The word *treats* got Felix's attention. He turned his jowly face in my direction and woofed softly.

Felix was a man of few words.

Once we were settled into our new abode, I called Will. When I'd filled him in on my change of plans and the reason behind it, he was silent for a few seconds.

"Maybe it's not such a great idea to get too involved with this guy," he finally said, "if robbing pawn shops is what he does for a living."

I looked around me as I lounged on the leather sofa in my own separate living room. "He's making a pretty fine living at it, if his house is any indicator. Hey," I sat up, "why did you say he robbed a pawn shop?"

"I was looking up the report as you were talking."

Of course you were, I thought but didn't say out loud. Will was sometimes an officer of the law first and human being second. But then again, to be fair, it was the middle of a weekday morning and I'd called him at his office, at the Collins County Sheriff's Department. I couldn't really blame him for being in sheriff mode.

I scanned the well-appointed room again. "Will, you should see his house. There's no way he's a petty thief."

"What *does* he do for a living?"

"He owns a construction company," I said. "Plus I think he gets military disability now."

"Which doesn't pay extremely well."

"His company's one of the biggest builders in the state, although I don't think he's been actively involved in running it since he got back from Afghanistan. Does he have a police record?" I knew darn well Will already had that info in front of him.

"He was active duty in his youth. Who knows what went down on military bases or overseas. But his civilian records show two DUIs in his late twenties and a couple of drunk and disorderlies. Since then, only a few speeding tickets. On country roads, on his motorcycle."

"Yeah, he said one time that bikers love to take the curves as fast as they dare."

"My guess is he's a bad boy who figured out by his thirties how to stay on the right side of the law."

The words *until now* hung unsaid in the air.

I stroked the soft leather of the sofa. *He's a bad boy who made good.* Again, I kept that thought to myself.

"That happens a lot," Will said. "Borderline criminal types who grow up just enough to learn how not to get caught."

I bristled. "Jake Black served two tours in Iraq and Afghanistan. He's hardly a, quote, 'borderline criminal type.'"

A pregnant pause. "Marcia, why do you always assume that because you like someone, they must be law-abiding?"

"Will," I said in my best snark voice, "why do you always assume that most people are *not* law-abiding?"

The sound in my ear of him blowing out air. I felt an echo of the tingle I get whenever he blows actual air into my ear while whispering little endearments. I decided to cut him some slack.

"Look," I said, "it's natural for people to assume others are law-abiding, until there is obvious evidence to the contrary." Then the snarky part of me added, "Unless you're law enforcement."

A beat of silence. I could see him in my mind's eye, shaking his head.

"Jake may have gotten into some trouble when he was young," I said, "but that doesn't mean he isn't basically a good guy."

Another sigh in my ear. "Promise me you'll stay out of this. *Please* remember that you're just the dog-sitter."

I rolled my eyes, even though Will couldn't see me. "Okay, I'm just the dog-sitter."

"Gotta go. Love you."

After the briefest of hesitations, I said, "Love you too."

I still choked a little on the words, which had nothing to do with Will and everything to do with why I was in counseling.

I disconnected and sank back into the buttery soft sofa.

What now?

A huge yawn suggested a nap was in order.

Midday naps were unheard of in my life. Normally I had two dogs in training at any given time, one close to done and one in the early stages, and I worked at least some part of almost every day.

But today had started particularly early. And I had nothing better to do, unless I wanted to check out what was on daytime TV.

A nap sounded much more desirable.

Will lay next to me on the sofa, trying to seduce me, but some dog kept barking in the distance.

Will blew in my ear, kissed my cheek, lowered his lips to my neck. I arched my body in his direction, making it easier for him to reach the sweet spot where neck and shoulder connect. A delicious shiver ran through me.

The dog barked again and Will froze. "Can't you make him be quiet."

I bristled, offended. It wasn't my fault that some dog was barking.

Will evaporated and I was enveloped in tan leather.

I fought my way to full consciousness and noted that leather made you sweaty if you slept on it. Good to know for future reference when I was as rich as the Blacks.

The dog was still barking.

I struggled to a sitting position. Buddy sat beside the sofa, worry in his eyes.

The barking dog had to be Felix and he was going ballistic.

I stumbled out of the guest suite, Buddy close on my heels, and followed the sound toward the back of the house.

Felix stood by the double sliding doors of the main living room, his nose pushed through the sheer curtains. He quivered all over, barking in short staccato bursts totally unlike his normal reserved woofs.

I was a bit shocked. I intentionally trained the natural territorialism out of my dogs, since they have to deal with strangers and even other dogs all the time in public.

But maybe Felix was feeling the need to defend the fortress in the absence of his master.

I came up beside him. "It's okay, boy," I said in a soft, reassuring voice.

He let out one more sharp bark, while staring at the freestanding garage. I held my hand up, palm outward, in a signal I teach all my dogs. It means stop what you're doing and wait for further guidance.

A short debate with myself. Take the dogs or not?

Fool, of course you shouldn't go investigate by yourself.

I opened the slider wide and gestured to Felix. He took off across the lawn. Buddy and I followed in his wake.

At first, the garage looked undisturbed, until I rounded the corner to the far side.

The window on that side, which had been intact earlier, now bore a big roundish hole in the middle, surrounded by jagged shards of glass. It was also open by about an inch. Had I missed that earlier?

I went back to the house and retrieved the key to the garage.

I unlocked the side door and found the switch for the overhead light. "Sit, boys."

Buddy obeyed but Felix was running in circles, sniffing the cement floor.

This dog needed some refresher training. I stepped over to him. "Felix!" I held my hand out, palm down—the signal that he was on duty and needed to pay attention.

He gave me a mournful look, then touched his nose to my palm.

"Good boy." Then I pointed to Buddy over near the door. "Sit."

Felix trotted over and sat down.

I made a circuit of the inside of the garage. There was no sign of an object—baseball, rock or whatever—that could have caused the hole in the window.

Everything seemed the same as it was before, but my gut was not happy. I made two more circuits of the space, looking for anything out of order. I wondered if my gut was just feeling at odds after being jerked awake from a nap.

I went outside, searching for a branch or something that might have blown against the window and broken it. Again, nothing.

With a shrug, I locked the side door of the garage. I headed back to the house, but noises from the street out front had me veering off toward the driveway.

I came to a halt. *Crapola!*

Felix started barking furiously. I lunged for his collar.

A plain beige sedan and two green and white sheriff's department cars were now parked in front of the property, one of the cruisers positioned across the end of the driveway. A phalanx of deputies and a couple of guys in plain clothes were marching toward us.

A man's voice yelled from beyond the cars, "Hey, what's going on here? You're blocking our driveway."

Relief washed through me as Felix tugged against my hand. I let him go. I too had recognized Jake Black's voice, coming from the passenger window of the white pickup that had just pulled up beside the police cars.

CHAPTER THREE

Jake had a hand on Felix's head, listing subtly in the dog's direction. Jake was a big guy, but Felix was a big dog. His face and body were all Bulldog but his legs were longer, probably from some distant Labrador, or maybe a Weimaraner, in his family tree. He came up to Jake's knee and had been trained to brace himself to take some of his master's weight.

Most likely only Janey and I knew that Jake was using the dog to maintain his balance, which would have been a lot easier if the dog were wearing his specialized service vest with its stabilizer bar for Jake to grab.

I considered going inside to find the vest, but Jake's body language had me worried.

His broad face was as red as I'd ever seen it. I was afraid he was about to have one of the "meltdowns" he'd told me about but I'd never witnessed. Anger control problems are common for people with traumatic brain injury.

The worry in Janey's pale blue eyes said she had the same concern. Shoving shoulder-length blonde hair, frizzy from the humidity, behind her ears, she placed a restraining hand on her husband's arm.

Jake shrugged her off. Not a good sign.

He snarled in the face of a dark-haired detective in an ill-fitting business suit. "I don't care how many pieces of paper you got from some judge. How dare you come in here like a bunch of storm troopers…" He spluttered to a stop as Janey once again tugged on the arm that wasn't using Felix for support.

He whirled on her—an even worse sign—and teetered dangerously on one foot.

Felix quickly shifted position and braced himself by spreading his legs. Once Jake seemed more stable on his feet, Felix leaned gently against his leg.

The maneuver, a type of deep pressure therapy, was meant to reduce anxiety, but it did little for Jake's anger.

The firm look in Janey's eyes did have an effect though. Jake froze, then took a deep breath.

"Come on inside," she said softly. "Let Detective Wright and his men do their jobs."

He patted her hand, just as the detective gestured to two deputies that they should head for the garage.

Jake pulled loose from his wife and followed as fast as he could, Felix keeping pace beside him. Detective Wright took off after him.

I followed in their wake, trying to decide whether I should report on the broken window in front of the officers or wait.

At the double-wide garage door, the detective gestured toward the big padlock and hasp on one side. "Unlock it."

Obviously reluctant, Jake produced a ring of keys and removed the padlock, then unlocked a lock in the middle of the roll-up door. The thunk of metal bars releasing inside.

One of the deputies grabbed the bottom of the door and shoved it up, exposing the Blacks' three motorcycles and the spotlessly clean workshop area.

A deputy began snapping pictures. "Bring in the trailer," Detective Wright said to another one.

Janey had caught up with us, huffing a little from the extra weight middle age had bestowed upon her. Her peaches-and-cream complexion paled to ghost white at the detective's words.

"Wha'?" Jake said, a bit slower to catch on to what was about to happen.

"We're impounding the bikes." Detective Wright waved

impatiently at one of the deputies in the driveway.

Jake's fists clenched. I could hear his teeth grinding from three feet away.

Both Janey and I jumped forward and grabbed his arms. Slugging a cop would not improve the situation.

Meanwhile, the detective was walking away, acting as if he hadn't been about to get flattened by a six-two, two-hundred-forty-pound combat vet. He crouched down beside one of the bikes, the black one. Then he gestured to the deputy with the camera and pointed to the side of the bike.

Jake moved forward, dragging us with him.

My eyes followed the detective's pointing finger to the rounded side of the gas tank, and a ragged long scratch in the black paint.

Jake's mouth fell open. "No!" he yelled.

I gestured toward the broken window. "Maybe whatever broke the window hit it."

Everybody's gaze turned to me, then to the window.

"When did that happen?" Janey said, a touch of wonder in her voice that some rock would dare to penetrate her husband's sanctum.

"Just before you all got here," I said. "I checked the outside of the garage earlier and that window was fine. Then Felix started barking and I came out and checked again and…"

The detective was glaring at me. "And you are?"

I gulped a little. "Marcia Banks, dog- and house-sitter." I told him what little more I knew, including about the guy getting into a white pickup, who might or might not have been hanging around the garage when I arrived.

He was a stony-faced audience but he did let me finish. And he did check the scratches around the lock on the side door, even had the deputy take pictures of them.

All this gave Jake time to calm down. That is until they began to load two of the motorcycles into the large trailer they'd backed into the driveway.

Again Janey and I grabbed his arms. "Let them take them,"

she hissed in his ear. "We've got no choice."

He let us hold him back while they loaded Janey's red three-wheeled bike—she said it was called a trike. I realized that indeed we were only holding him with his permission when he suddenly shook us loose like we were an old shirt he was shedding. "Wait!" He stepped forward.

Felix was beside him in a flash.

I indulged in a moment of maternal pride. *That's my boy, doin' his job!*

Jake was pointing to the black leather bag on the side of his black bike, which was halfway up the ramp. "That's not my saddlebag."

The detective held up a hand and the two deputies who'd been rolling the bike up the ramp between them stopped.

Jake walked around the ramp to the other side, Felix practically glued to his jeans leg. "This one too. They're not my bags."

The detective stepped forward and made a show of examining the bag on our side. Then he snapped on blue latex gloves, like those the deputies handling the bike were wearing. He leaned forward, tentatively touched the end of what looked like scrape marks in the leather.

He held his finger up close to his face, rubbed it and his thumb together. A few grains of sand caught the sunlight as they drifted to the pavement.

He gestured to a third deputy. "Put a bag around all that." He pointed to the saddlebag. "We need to analyze the sand."

Now that he mentioned it, I could see some tawny grains embedded in the leather.

"That's not my bag," Jake said emphatically. "Janey get the photo from the living room."

I knew which one he meant. I'd noticed three photos earlier, front and center on the mantel. Their wedding picture had caught my eye first, with Janey standing tall and proud, forty pounds lighter and drop-dead gorgeous. On the right of it was their daughter, Andrea, smiling and holding a high-school diploma, and on the left, Jake, fifteen years younger and grinning like a kid on Christmas as he stood next to a shiny black bike.

This bike in front of us.

Janey took off at a trot for the house. She was well padded, but she could move pretty fast when motivated.

Buddy and I should have followed. This really wasn't my business. But I didn't move.

Curiosity killed the cat. My mother's voice in my head.

She had a point. My curiosity…okay, my nosiness, had gotten me into trouble more than once. I figured that if I were that proverbial cat, I had about four of my nine lives left.

Janey returned with the photo.

Jake grabbed it and stuck it under the detective's nose, then threatened to take out said nose by jabbing at the picture with a large index finger. "There! *Those* are *my* bags."

I craned to see but couldn't make out more than a blur of black and tan, and the younger Jake's big grin. My throat closed. Life hadn't treated him all that well since then.

The detective looked at the picture and then at Jake. "Side bags can be changed."

Then he broke Jake's heart and endangered his own life by confiscating the photo.

CHAPTER FOUR

Jake let Janey and me haul him back away from the detective. He was grinding his teeth, but his chest was heaving, as if he were fighting back sobs.

Once he was calm enough to leave him to Janey's care alone, I did go back into the house. I couldn't watch the pain on his face as they carted his bike away.

Inside, more deputies were searching the rooms. Most of them were being neat, but one guy started pulling sofa cushions off and tossing them about.

"Hey," an older, heavy-set deputy said in a sharp voice, "show some respect."

I found myself drawn in his direction. "Do you know Jake?"

His blue eyes, under shaggy gray brows, bore into me. But then his face softened. "Yeah, we ride together."

It took me a second to realize he meant on motorcycles.

His presence explained the neater than usual behavior of cops executing a search warrant. Perhaps this deputy, who had several strips on his sleeves, had told the others about Jake's service record.

I glanced at his name tag. *Sergeant Phelps*.

Buddy and I left him and his comrades to their work and went into the guest suite. Whoever had searched here hadn't been as careful. With a sigh, I began to straighten the room.

I was dismayed to find that they'd searched my duffle bag. I tried not to think about strange male hands pawing through my underwear.

But I just about blew when I went into the bathroom and found Buddy's kibble had been dumped on the floor. Seething, I scooped most of it back into its bag. Fortunately, Janey kept a spotless house. The floor literally was clean enough to eat off of.

I signaled to Buddy that it was okay for him to eat up the few stray bits, while I worked on reining in my temper. Janey and Jake had enough problems without my anger adding fuel to the fire.

It took another hour for the deputies and detectives to finish their search—did I mention it's a big house? There was a second plainclothes guy, also dark-haired but shorter and older. He hadn't said a word the whole time, but his eyes darted around, taking in everything.

The younger one, Detective Wright, stepped forward and handed Jake a piece of paper. "Here's a list of what we're taking."

Janey craned to read it around Jake's big shoulder. Her eyes teared up. "My jewelry?" she choked out. Jake crumpled the paper in his fist.

The doorbell rang.

"I'll get it," I chirped and scrambled away, Buddy following. I was tired of trying to hold Jake back from creaming this detective. He deserved to be creamed.

Out of the corner of my eye, I saw the quiet one step forward. "You'll get it all back, ma'am," he said in a soothing voice.

"Unless it's stolen property," his partner said, but not until he'd taken several steps backward, out of Jake's reach.

I swallowed a grin. The guy had some sense of self-preservation after all.

The doorbell rang again. I yanked the door open.

And there stood Will, looking tall, tired and handsome in his slightly rumpled khaki sheriff's uniform. His baby blues lit up in his rugged face. "Hey."

"What are you doing here?" I blurted out.

His face fell. "We had a date, remember?"

Crapola. It had slipped my mind that I'd invited him to spend the weekend with me, in my cheap motel room near the beach.

Fortunately, he'd crouched down to say hi to Buddy via a vigorous scratch behind his ears, giving me time to recover.

"Sure, yeah." I plastered on a big smile, trying to figure out how to break it to him that I didn't feel comfortable having a male friend stay the night in a client's guest suite. Maybe the motel room was still available.

"How'd you find us?" I said.

He straightened to a stand. "GPS."

Duh. He'd looked up Jake's record. No doubt there was an address in there somewhere.

He held the ten-gallon hat that was part of his uniform in his hand. Sweat had darkened his hair almost to black and plastered it on his forehead. One end of his mouth quirked up. "Mind if I come in out of the heat?"

"Oh, sorry." I stepped back, then whispered, "But…"

I didn't have to finish my warning. His head swiveled around, taking in the scene—the deputies standing around, the subtle upheaval of a room well searched even though the searchers had tried to be neat about it, and the tension in the tableau of detectives facing off with Jake and Janey. "Crapola, as you would say," he whispered back.

I gave him a small smile, genuine this time. "They were just leaving."

Once the police were gone, the transformation in Jake was amazing. He settled on the sofa, an arm draped around Janey's shoulders, the other hand running over his buzz-cut light brown hair. Felix dropped to the floor at his feet.

Jake gave Will and me, still standing near the door, a friendly smile.

I reminded myself that this easy-going personality was the real Jake. The quick, hard-to-control temper, along with his balance problems, were due to the injuries he'd suffered when an Army supply truck hit an IED on a dirt road in Afghanistan. It blew with such force that Jake's jeep behind it was flipped into a ditch.

After I'd introduced Will, Jake gestured to a couple of arm-chairs. "Have a seat."

Will jammed his hat under his arm, stood at attention and gave him a mock salute. "Thank you, *Mister* Black."

Jake chuckled. "At ease, Sheriff. I see you've been check-ing up on me."

I looked at Will, then Jake, then back at Will.

Will picked up on my confusion. His sensitivity to my moods is one of the things I love about him—most of the time.

"Your friend Jake here was a warrant officer," he explained, "during his latest tour in the Corp of Engineers. They're addressed as *Mister* rather than a rank." He lowered himself into one of the proffered chairs. "But in the records from his first go-round with the Army, there's an Article 15."

"What's that?" I took the other armchair, across from his. Buddy sidled up beside me. I stroked his head and silky ears.

"It's like pleading no-contest in a civilian court," Will said. "You accept your punishment without admission of guilt."

Jake was still smiling, his body relaxed. "There were quite a few Article 15's in those early years, but most of them got expunged when I was discharged. That one was field grade, harder to get rid of."

Will nodded as if he knew what all that meant.

Jake's smile broadened into a grin. "There's a funny story behind it. I was stationed in Germany at the time. Me and some boys got ourselves plastered one night in the NCO club, and one of 'em dared me to steal a jeep. Liked to killed myself climbing the fence into the motor pool, but I got to that ole jeep and started it up. I wasn't plannin' on goin' anywhere with it, since the motor pool gate was locked up tight, but my foot slipped off the brake and next thing I knew I'd sideswiped the Colonel's Mercedes." He chuckled again and slapped his thigh.

"Was it a funny story then?" Will asked, his face dead serious.

I squirmed in my chair.

"Yeah, it was actually," Jake's expression sobered some, "until my CO quietly suggested I take an honorable discharge rather than re-upping again. I'd planned to be an Army lifer, although I wasn't too happy at the time that they'd made me a grunt worker for the engineers."

Jake gave his wife's shoulders a squeeze. "But all things happen for a reason, as they say. When I got out, I married Janey here and then started up my little construction company."

I snorted softly under my breath. Jake's "little" construction company was now a multi-million-dollar corporation. I knew the rest of the story. Believing his country needed him, Jake had re-enlisted eight years ago and had been deployed to the Middle East. I secretly suspected a desire for adventure had fueled that decision along with patriotism.

Will was staring at Jake, his profile toward me. I couldn't see all of his face, but his mouth was down-turned.

To break up the tension emanating from him, I asked, "So, what is a field grade article whatever?"

"It's one answering a charge by a field grade officer," Jake said, "a major or above." He looked at Will. "Hey, you must have an in with somebody in the Army, to get your hands on those records."

"I know a couple of people at Camp Blanding," Will said, his voice neutral.

With a jolt, I realized how he'd come to know those people, last spring when he was helping to chase down one of my clients' rapist turned stalker, who'd turned out to be stationed at Blanding. I shuddered. That guy had given *sexist* a whole new meaning for me.

Will glanced my way. After a beat, he took a deep breath and his body relaxed some.

He turned back to Jake. "No problems getting out on bail?"

Jake let out a sharp bark of laughter. "Man, you don't mince words, do you, Sheriff?"

Janey leaned forward, her eyes hard in her round face. "Sir, you are in our home."

"Now, now, Janey." Jake patted her arm. "The sheriff's just bein' protective of Marcia here. He wants to know if we really are armed robbers, that's all."

I sucked in air. I'd been thinking the robbery was a snatch-and-run affair. *Armed* was much more serious.

"No, Sheriff," Jake said, "I didn't have any trouble making bail, and no we didn't rob that pawn shop." He waved a hand around in the air. "Does it look like I need to rob people."

That curious cat popped up its furry little head and I blurted out, "What did happen, Jake?"

"Best I can tell…" He squinted his eyes at Will. "Johnny Law ain't always all that forthcoming. But it seems two people robbed a pawn shop in a shopping center that we go to a lot—the shopping center, not the pawn shop, although we do know the owners. The robbers had ski masks on but it was a man and woman, built like me and Janey, and they took off on bikes kinda like ours. One was black, and the other a red trike like Janey's."

"The black one had a sidecar?" I asked. That would be one huge coincidence.

Jake shook his head and opened his mouth, but Janey jumped in. "We tried and tried to tell them that Jake can't ride two wheels anymore, but they weren't buying it."

"Kept saying I must've gotten better in recent times but was pretending to still have balance problems." Jake shook his head again. "Dang hard to prove a negative."

"What do you mean?" I asked.

"How do I prove I'm not faking?"

I saw his point. Every time he swayed or stumbled, they could say he was doing it on purpose. But I knew better. A little over a year ago, I'd trained Felix specifically to be his living crutch when needed, in addition to the responses I taught all my dogs to help with PTSD symptoms.

Prior to that, Jake had required a walker to keep from falling, which was humiliating as all get out for a macho man like him, who was only in his mid-forties. And he hadn't been able to ride his beloved motorcycle, until Janey came up with the idea of a sidecar for Felix.

Getting the dog comfortable with riding in the open car had been another challenge, but it had been worth it to see Jake's gleeful face the first time he took himself and Felix for a spin around the block.

"Hey, I'm hungry," Will said, interrupting my reverie. "You ready to go?"

"Sure. Let me grab my purse." I stood. "I'll move my things to a motel later," I said to Jake and Janey.

"Why?" Jake said. "Thought this was solvin' some problem for you."

"Well, yeah." I explained briefly about the drywood termites and the roof.

"Why spend money on a motel?" Janey said. "You're welcome here for as long as you need to stay."

"Well, thanks." I glanced at Will. He didn't look happy. "Uh, don't wait up for me," I said to the Blacks.

"You'll need keys then." Janey stood and headed for the kitchen, making a beeline for the Army helmet key rack by the back door.

I followed her. "I've got the ones out of the fake rock."

"Okay. I'll put these back in the rock then." She lifted off a ring with two keys on it. "Leftovers from when Jake first came home and was so forgetful. He kept losing his keys, so I got several sets made."

If it had been me, I would have changed the locks, with multiple sets of keys floating around out there in the world. But then I'm from the big city up North, not a small town like Buckland Beach, Florida.

Will and I settled in at a wooden picnic table on the deck of a beachside restaurant. Buddy wiggled under the table and laid down at my feet.

Once again, I was grateful for the many outdoor dining

opportunities in Florida that solved the problem of what to do with one's dog. Even in winter, leaving a dog in a car wasn't an option, with the intense Florida sun. When I had a dog in training that was one thing, and the restaurant staff had to allow me to bring a dog in a service vest inside. But I wasn't disabled and technically Buddy wasn't a service dog anymore—he was my mentor dog.

After we'd ordered enough fried seafood to clog our arteries for life, I cleared my throat. "Look, I know you have no reason to trust Jake–"

"No, I don't," Will said in a harsh tone. "And I don't like the idea of you staying there."

I bristled and sucked in air through my nose. Letting it out slowly, I said, "I know these people, Will. You don't. You're going to have to trust me on this."

He opened his mouth, then his eyes clouded. He clamped his mouth shut again.

The waitress saved the moment by delivering our appetizer of fried gator tail.

I dipped one in the savory sauce and practically swallowed it whole. The next one I actually chewed for a few seconds. It was sooo good.

And no, it doesn't taste like chicken. More a gamier, chewier version of lobster tail.

I finished off my half before I bothered to look up.

Will was watching me, an indulgent expression on his face. "Hungry a little?"

"I never got any lunch." I eyed the last two breaded clumps on the plate, knowing they were rightfully Will's.

He picked up one of them, dipped it in the tiny cup of sauce, held it in front of his open mouth. Then he grinned. "Take the last one."

I didn't give him a chance to change his mind.

I wiped my greasy fingers on my napkin and looked up. The indulgent grin had faded.

"Seriously, Marcia." He pronounced my name slowly, emphasizing each syllable—Mar-see-a. "You don't know that these people aren't responsible for these robberies. You really need to stay out of it."

I just sat there, not sure what to say.

"And by the way, what happened to our romantic getaway at the beach?" His baby blues bore into me.

I stared at the top of his head, at his short brown hair, streaked with gold from the Florida sun.

My eyes drifted south, to his rugged face, then the broad shoulders and chest filling out his rumpled khaki uniform shirt. That chest narrowed down to slender hips and lean but muscular legs, both currently hidden from my view by the table between us.

That table might as well be the Gulf of Mexico.

I knew I was darn lucky to have this man in my life, and I was also just as sure that I was about to blow that good deal.

CHAPTER FIVE

The waitress delivered our fried shrimp, hush puppies, French fries, and the small nod to nutrition in the form of a tiny bowl of homemade cole slaw.

We ate in silence for few minutes.

Then Will cleared his throat. "Look, the sheriff here had to have a good bit of evidence against Black in order to arrest him, *and* get the warrants to search his house and impound his bikes."

"Yeah, but most of that evidence is based on some witness's account that they saw Jake's and Janey's bikes leaving the scene. There's no way that Jake Black could ride his bike without the sidecar."

Will shrugged.

"He has traumatic brain injury." I heard my voice rising and stopped, gulped a little for air.

I shouldn't be talking about a client's medical diagnosis anyway, but Janey had indicated that they'd already told the local sheriff's people about Jake's condition.

"He could've recovered more than he's letting on," Will said.

I took a deep breath, trying to calm myself. "I researched TBI when I was working with him last year. His injury was pretty serious, and recovery is not that fast. Usually it takes two years, and even then there are often residual symptoms."

Will lifted one shoulder. "Usually." He grabbed a couple of fries and stuffed them in his face.

I wanted to slug him.

I took another deep breath, and let it out very, very slowly. "Will, I know it is your nature, as a law enforcement officer, to be skeptical. But if you value our relationship, you will keep an open mind here." I paused for dramatic effect. "I *know* these people and *you* don't."

He looked a bit startled. Then he reached out and covered my hand on the table.

I resisted the urge to poke the back of his hand with my fork.

"Okay," he said. Then after a pause, he added, "it's not my jurisdiction anyway."

We ate in not-so-companionable silence after that.

When our plates were obviously devastated, the waitress appeared and asked about dessert.

We both shook our heads in unison.

While we waited for her to bring the check, Will asked again, "What happened to our romantic getaway?"

"I'm so sorry, Will…" I trailed off, not sure how to begin to apologize for the shift from awesome getaway to local sheriff's department investigation. I was also very cognizant of my finances. Free room and board sure beat out a hundred dollars a night in a second-rate beachside motel.

He smiled, revealing his dimples. "If this mess isn't straightened out by tomorrow night, how about I spring for a night at the beachfront motel?"

My heart fluttered. This man was far kinder to me than I deserved, and boy, did I love those dimples.

I returned his smile. "I'd like that. If I'd been thinking straight this morning, I would've kept the reservation anyway, but I thought I'd be dog-sitting tonight."

He shrugged. "I'm learning to expect the unexpected where you're concerned."

I wasn't sure how to take that comment, so I ignored it. "I hate sending you home. You look tired and it's such a long drive."

He gave a slight shake of his head. "The drive here isn't that much longer than to your place. It's a fairly straight shot across from Collinsville." He devoured his last hush puppy in one bite. "Don't let yourself get dragged into this, Marcia. It's the Blacks' problem, not yours."

"Oh, don't worry. I'm just taking advantage of the free roof over my–" Buddy shifted under the table and rested his chin on my knee. "Over our heads."

"Promise?" Will asked.

"I promise." But my fingers may have been a little bit crossed as I scratched behind Buddy's ear under the table.

I might have kept that promise though, if I hadn't stumbled on the Buckland County Sheriff's Department the next morning, as Buddy and I were exploring our new home away from home.

When I saw the sign, my arms turned the steering wheel of the car before I'd really thought it through.

Buddy and I walked into the welcome coolness of the lobby. The room looked a lot like a doctor's office waiting area, only less welcoming—beige tile floor, beige walls, a reception window in one of the walls. The only spot of color was the orange vinyl on the chairs around the perimeter.

A female deputy slid the glass open in the window. "Can I help you?" she asked in a heavy Southern accent. Not Floridian though, more likely Georgian.

"Sergeant Phelps, please."

She gave Buddy a skeptical look. "He a service dog?"

He wasn't wearing his vest and I could have lied, but I didn't like to go there when I didn't have to. "Yes and no. I'm a service dog trainer and he's my mentor dog. I happened to have him with me, and it's too hot to leave him in the car."

She gave a brisk nod. "Have a seat an' I'll see if the sergeant's in."

I wandered away, scanning the photos of sheriffs, past and present, that covered one of the walls.

The deputy talked into a phone receiver in low tones, her eyes following me as if she expected me to steal something. But portraits of gray-haired men with middle-aged spread straining the buttons of their dark green uniform shirts were not all that tempting.

I stopped in front of the photo of the one woman in the group. She was downright petite, with dark blonde hair pulled back in a no-nonsense ponytail. I glanced down at her name, but the date caught my eye first—*2014 to…* The spot after "to" was blank. She was the current sheriff, midway through her first term.

Good for you… I searched again for her name… *Sheriff Tabitha Baker.*

Tabby? Seriously? my snarky inner voice said. *She got elected with that name?*

The feminist in me grabbed an imaginary two-by-four and smacked Ms. Snarky upside the head with it.

Buddy's ears perking—the signal that someone was approaching—jerked me away from the cat fight in my mind's eye.

Then he shifted between me and the footsteps on the tile floor behind me.

I turned and raised my eyes to meet those of the heavy-set sergeant from Jake's living room the previous day. I noticed that his thick hair and eyebrows weren't all gray after all. The gray hairs were mixed in with blond ones.

He tilted his head toward the glass window. "Shelley Ann'll be happier if we take your dog outside." He made an after-you gesture in the direction of the front door.

I used the minute or so that it took to walk outside to think up an opening. "I'm concerned about Mr. Black," I said, once we were standing on the scorching hot sidewalk. "Can you tell me where things stand with the investigation?"

Phelps arched an eyebrow at me, then turned and led the way around to the side of the building, to a small shaded area. He took out a pack of cigarettes and lit one up.

"He's a war hero," I added, although this wasn't technically true. Jake had been in the Corp of Engineers, building bridges and barracks. But as far as I was concerned, anybody who was willing to go to a war zone so that I could sit home feeling safe was a hero.

"Can't talk about an ongoing investigation," the sergeant finally said, his tone brusque. "But I *can* say that Jake Black needs all the help he can get."

Okay, this felt like some kind of code.

"What kind of help?" I asked tentatively.

"The robbers were definitely bikers. They knew how to handle those bikes. The guy, his bike went down while he was turning out of the parking lot. Musta hit some gravel or sand. He was back on his feet, had that bike up and was out of there before anybody could even react."

My jaw was hanging open. "Surely you all realize that Jake can't do all that. He can't even ride on two wheels anymore, much less pick a motorcycle up off the ground, jump on it and take off."

My mind flashed to the detective yesterday, rubbing sand particles between his fingers, saying they'd have to get it analyzed. So that's what that was all about. He thought the sand came from that parking lot exit.

The sergeant didn't say anything, but his eyes had softened as he took another drag on his cigarette.

"Jake claims those aren't his saddle bags," I said.

The sergeant shrugged, took a last drag, then dropped the cigarette on the sidewalk. "Best bet is to find out who really did it. The other bikers around here might know."

"So, why aren't you all talking to them?"

He shrugged again, ground out the butt with his toe. "You oughta talk to Larry."

"Who's Larry?"

"He's one of the bikers. He can tell you about the others."

"And why should I talk to this guy," I said, "or the bikers?"

He just stared at me, his blue eyes narrowed and intense under bushy eyebrows, his thick lips clamped together in a tight line.

I swallowed back a sigh. "Where can I find him?"

"In the phone book. Lawrence Merrick, Esquire."

It took a beat for that to compute. "He's a lawyer?"

"Yup." The sergeant's eyes bore into mine for a long moment, then he turned on his heel and marched off toward the front of the building.

I looked down at Buddy. "Okay, that was maybe the strangest conversation I've ever had."

Buddy tilted his head in his patented what's-up look.

I had barely finished strapping him into his safety harness in my car and had settled into the driver's seat when my friend Becky called.

"Hey, what's up?" she chirped cheerfully in my ear. "How's life at the beach?"

I started the car. "Um, I'm not on the beach exactly…" I switched the call over to my Bluetooth and, as I headed back to Jake and Janey's place, I filled her in on where I was staying and why.

"Speaking of romantic getaways," I said, "how's the honeymoon going? And why are you calling me when you should be gazing into Andy's lovely brown eyes?"

It was a total irony that Becky, who had perfected casual dating and short-term flings, had fallen like a rock when she'd come over to help me paint my house last spring. Will had also come to help—indeed he'd organized the whole thing. And he'd brought another helper, a light-skinned African-American named Andy Matthews, who'd recently become one of Will's deputies in Collins County.

After a whirlwind romance, Becky and Andy had quietly married, with Will and me as the only witnesses, and they were now honeymooning in the Bahamas.

"He's taking a swim. I didn't feel like getting wet this early in the day, so I'm lying on a chaise lounge watching him do laps." I visualized her lying on said chaise, her perfect hourglass figure in a bikini, dark curls framing her heart-shaped face. The only thing that kept me from hating this woman was that she was the nicest person I'd ever met.

"But getting back to this robbery..." Becky's voice shifted from lazy drawl to worried friend. "You're not going to get involved, are you?"

"Well, I wasn't planning to but I just had a rather odd conversation with a member of the local sheriff's department."

I was pulling up in front of Jake and Janey's house by the time I'd repeated the gist of that conversation, including the strange boring-into-my-head look the sergeant had given me.

"Hmm," Becky said. "Sounds like he was trying to tell you something, without actually saying it out loud."

"Yeah, that was my take on it. But what was he trying to tell me?"

"He seems to be encouraging you to investigate on your own."

"Which is totally bizarre." I flashed on Will's frowning face. "Law enforcement does not normally encourage meddling from civilians."

"Maybe he's concerned about his biker buddy," Beck said, "because he knows about something rotten going on in the sheriff's department."

I shrugged, even though she couldn't see me. That seemed like a bit of a leap. "Or," I said, "that detective is so intent on proving a case against Jake that he isn't even bothering to pursue other angles."

"Are you going to call this Merrick guy?" Becky asked.

"Probably." I didn't have anything better to do, since my romantic weekend had evaporated on me. I wondered briefly why I hadn't heard from Will this morning.

Becky sighed on the other end of the line. "I know better than to try and talk you out of this, so just be careful, okay? I'm not in the mood to break in a new best friend when I have a new husband to train right now."

I laughed out loud. "Don't let Andy hear you say that."

She giggled. "Oh, don't worry. I won't."

We signed off, and Buddy and I climbed out of the car and went to the front door. Jake's truck wasn't in the driveway so no big surprise when no one answered the doorbell. I dug out my keys and let us in.

A note was propped up on the coffee table. *Jake and Felix went for a ride. I'm grocery shopping. Back in a while. Make yourself at home.* It was signed *Janey.*

How could he have gone for a ride? Then I remembered the other bike, the dark blue one that the detectives hadn't taken. I guessed the sidecar worked on that one as well.

I had my laptop with me but hadn't yet had a chance to get the wifi network code from Jake or Janey, so I went looking for an old-fashioned phone book.

I found it, upside down in a drawer next to the junk drawer in the kitchen, a rather thin volume, covering all of Buckland County. I didn't have to flip through it to find Lawrence Merrick. He was plastered on the back cover. He was lean and handsome with a boyish face, probably late thirties, his brown eyes serious. His pose replicated ones I'd seen before in lawyer ads, "caught" in the act of rolling up his sleeves to get to work on your case. The rather unoriginal slogan under it read, *Need a lawyer. Call Larry. He's on your side.*

"Of course you are," I muttered under my breath, "if I'm paying you to be."

Buddy looked up at me, his head cocked to one side.

I called the number that was printed in bright red across the bottom of the phone book cover.

"Larry Merrick. How can I help?" His voice was chipper.

"Uh, hi." I wasn't really expecting to get the man himself right out of the gate, especially on a Saturday. Was the number in the ad his cell phone? "Um, my name is Marcia Banks. I'm a friend of Jake Black's."

"Awesome. Jake's a good dude."

"Well, he's in some trouble at the moment. Haven't you heard?"

He hadn't, so I filled him in.

"Oh man, that sucks. Does he need representation?"

"Um, no. I'm calling because someone suggested that you could fill me in on the bikers in the area. You see I don't believe Jake did it."

"Okay, but I don't really understand how I can help." His voice had turned a bit wary.

I glanced at my watch. It was a little after eleven. "Hey, can I take you out to lunch or something? Pick your brain some about motorcycle gangs?"

"Clubs, ma'am. Not gangs." Now he sounded offended.

"Oh, what's the difference?"

"Gangs are criminals who happen to ride motorcycles. Most bikers are law-abiding citizens."

"See, that's the kind of stuff I need to know, in order to help Jake and Janey."

"Okay, tell ya what. I know the folks who own that pawn shop. Not well mind you, but I've done some legal work for them. Let's meet there and we can talk to them, and then go to lunch and you can ask your questions."

"Wow, that would be great."

"I've got something to do first. I'll meet you there at twelve-thirty, okay?" He gave me directions to the pawn shop.

I disconnected, then wondered how a busy lawyer could just drop everything to meet me like that. I glanced down at his ad on the phone book. Then again, maybe he wasn't all that busy.

He'd also told me that the strip shopping center where the pawn shop was located was only ten minutes from Jake's house. So I had time for a snack, since lunch would be delayed. I took Janey at her word about making myself at home and grabbed an apple from the fridge.

Then I freshened up and wrote a note for Jake and Janey. Refilling Buddy's water bowl, I put it in the guest bathroom.

Dogs complicated things when entering business establishments and restaurants. I crouched down and explained to him that I'd be back in a couple of hours.

He just cocked his head to one side.

Ten minutes later, I slowed my car, searching for the shopping center's entrance among the multitude of signs and driveways into the commercial enterprises along this section of road.

Florida State Road A1A is an unusual thoroughfare that runs right along the east coast of the state, from just south of the Georgia border to Key West. In places, it resembles a country road, only with the Atlantic on one side, but as it passes through the many beach towns along the coast, it becomes a slow-moving and sometimes clogged Main Street.

It was a good thing that I'd slowed down, because the white pickup coming out of the shopping center's parking lot didn't.

It roared out onto the road, swerving briefly into my lane. As it blasted past me, I caught a quick glimpse of the two people inside the cab. I couldn't tell if they were male or female because they wore ski masks.

In Florida. In September.

CHAPTER SIX

Heart pounding, I circled the parking lot, looking for a space but also debating if I should call the police. I found a spot not far from the storefront with the sign *Belenky's Fine Jewelry and Collectibles* over the door. In smaller black letters under that was *Pawn Broker ~ We buy estate jewelry.*

I got out and jogged to the door, my stomach queasy from nerves. A cheerful little bell dinged as I pushed the door open. No one was in sight.

"Hello," I called out.

No response other than the Musak playing softly. It calmed my heart rate some.

I moved down one of the aisles toward the back of the shop, eyeing the eclectic array of merchandise—everything from guitars to weed-whackers on one side and locked displays of smaller, more expensive-looking items, mostly jewelry, on the other.

Across the back of the shop stretched a counter with a cash register. My heart kicked up another couple of notches when I got a good look at the glass case under the counter. No doubt it had contained more jewelry or something of equal value. But it was now empty, the glass on the front of it smashed in.

I pivoted, ready to bolt, when I heard a moan. I froze, my eyes darting around the shop for any signs of human presence.

Another moan, from behind the counter.

I inched forward and peeked over. A thin, gray-haired woman lay on the floor.

I raced around and stooped down. "Ma'am, are you alright?"

Dumb question, Banks!

I quickly fumbled my phone out of my pocket and punched 911, told the dispatcher the address and then yelled, "Hurry! A woman's hurt, really bad."

"Is she alive?" the dispatcher asked. "Do you know how to check her pulse?"

Without thinking, I stuffed my phone back in my pocket. Ignoring the garbled noises coming from it, I gently slid a hand under the woman's head to tilt it back slightly so I could feel for a pulse on her neck. Liquid, warm and sticky, oozed between my fingers.

I gagged, then swallowed hard. The fingers of my other hand were desperately seeking a pulse. Finally, they found it, weak and uneven.

"Ma'am, can you hear me?"

Her eyelids fluttered open. "Not… no…"

I leaned closer to her mouth.

"No…n-nuh not…ache b-back." Her body stiffened and she grimaced, closing her eyes.

"Don't try to talk, ma'am." Distant sirens penetrated my brain. "Help is on the way."

Her eyes fluttered open again, then they went wide, staring sightlessly past my face. "No… black! Don't…" And she passed out.

I eased her head down onto the floor, slid my hand out from under it and stared at the blood on my fingers.

A scraping sound behind me. I jumped to my feet, whirled around, and almost collided with the guy from the cover of the phone book.

"Ms. Banks?" he said with a smile. Then his gaze went to the bloody hand I was holding out in front of me. It was less than an inch from the lapel of his gray suit.

His eyes went wide and he stepped back. Then his gaze dropped to the woman on the floor and his face paled.

"I found her that way," I quickly said.

The sirens were louder.

"Look," I said, "can you go out front and flag down the paramedics?"

He shook his head. "No, *you* go out front." His expression said that he thought I would finish the old lady off if I was left alone with her.

But I didn't really care what he thought. Because I suddenly desperately needed to get out of there, before I threw up all over a crime scene.

The quieter of the two detectives from the previous day turned out to be the one in charge. He introduced himself as Lieutenant Harrison when he entered the stark interview room where I'd been cooling my heels for a good fifty minutes. And this after standing around, answering questions at the shopping center for what seemed like hours.

"Would you like something to drink?" the lieutenant asked. "Some water perhaps?"

"No thanks." I was parched—and starving, lunch never had happened—but I just wanted to get out of there and go home to Buddy. Or rather back to the Blacks' house.

The lieutenant sat across from me and folded his hands on the table in front of him. "You told the responding officer that you saw a white pickup truck leaving as you came into the lot?"

I nodded numbly, hating the fact that my words incriminated Jake and Janey.

He made me run through the damning story again. When I got to the part where I'd found the old lady, he stopped me. "What were her words exactly?"

I stared at the ceiling, trying to remember. So much had happened so fast, and I'd been more focused on willing her to stay alive until the paramedics got there.

"She said no a few times… um, one of them might have been *not*. And at one point she said something about her back hurting."

"Exact words, please."

I scrunched up my face, straining to remember. "'No, no, not'… and then 'ache back.' And then she closed her eyes. She seemed to be in a lot of pain." Suddenly my eyes stung and my throat wouldn't let more words out. I swallowed hard. "Is she okay?"

His face softened. "We'll talk about that in a minute. What else did she say?"

I took a deep breath. "Her eyes opened again but she didn't seem to be looking at me. She had that glazed look when somebody's remembering something from the past. Her eyes went real wide and she clearly said, 'No,' and then either 'back' or 'black'…" Okay, I was fudging some. I wanted it to be back, not black. "And then 'don't' and she passed out."

I stared at him, not able to get my question out a second time.

His eyes were sympathetic. He slowly shook his head.

Dear God! The woman was dead.

And her dying words sure seemed to implicate Jake Black.

I picked my phone up off the table. "Uh, can I make a call? I need to make arrangements for my dog. He's been cooped up in the house most of the day."

"At the Blacks' house? Yours the big black one with the tan markings?"

My stomach clenched. "Yes."

"He and the other dog were taken to Animal Services."

"What?" I screeched. I jumped out of my chair. "You had no right to do that."

He held out his hands, made a sit-down gesture which I ignored. "We had an incident a few years ago. A dog died because his owners were arrested and there wasn't anybody else living there to take care of him. Now we have a strict policy that we can't leave an animal unattended when we arrest someone."

I looked at my watch. It was four-twenty. Even on Saturdays, most county pounds were open until five, to accommodate weekend pet adopters.

But my car was still back at the shopping center. And if I didn't get there in time today, I wouldn't be able to get Buddy back until Monday, or maybe Tuesday, if they closed on Monday to make up for Saturday.

"Ms. Banks, please sit down." The lieutenant's voice was a bit firmer than it had been.

"Didn't the Blacks tell you that I was staying there?"

"Yes, but we still had to take the dogs, just in case…"

I swallowed hard as the implications of that sank in. In case I was arrested too.

The lieutenant made the sit-down gesture again.

"No. I'm a witness, not a suspect." I hoped to God that was true. "You can't hold me. I have to go get my dog." I was madder than I'd ever been, even madder than the night I found out my then husband had been cheating on me.

I headed for the door, but the lieutenant stepped in front of me.

"Let me out of here. Now!" I shoved through gritted teeth.

"Your dog is fine. I told the officer to explain that they are both valuable service dogs."

That did little to calm my pounding heart. I had this irrational need to get to Buddy immediately. But I had no transportation and the only people I knew in this town were no doubt in one of the other interview rooms, or in a jail cell by now.

I felt intensely alone, helpless, and that only made me madder.

"I said, let me out of here." A low snarl that I hardly recognized as my own voice.

The lieutenant's face pinched into an unreadable expression, but he reached behind him and opened the door. "I may be by later to ask some more questions," was his parting shot.

I raced down a corridor, looking for the way out.

A man stepped into my path. "Hey, Ms. Banks."

It took me a second to recognize the lawyer, Larry Merrick.

"You need a ride back to your car?" he asked.

"Oh yes." I almost threw my arms around him and kissed him, but caught myself at the last second. "You're a godsend."

He led the way out of the police station and to a light blue SUV. Gallantly holding the door open for me, he made an after-you gesture.

I bit my tongue to keep from saying, *Cut the chivalry crap and take me to my car.*

Once he was in the driver's seat, he seemed to take forever to get his seatbelt untwisted and clicked into place, then he adjusted the vents and turned the radio volume down.

"How far is the shopping center?" I asked, hoping to convey that I was in a hurry. "I wasn't really paying attention when the officer brought me here."

"About fifteen minutes from here." He pointed to his left, then finally put the vehicle in gear and started backing out of the parking space.

"And do you happen to know how far the county animal services' office is from there?"

He pulled up to the exit of the sheriff's department's parking lot. "Hmm, it's ten minutes from here the other way, so about twenty-five minutes."

"Mr. Merrick," I struggled to keep my voice calm, "could you possibly take me there first. They've got my dog, and Jake's. I'm afraid I won't be able to get back in time before they close."

"I guess. Sure." He flipped his blinker over to go right instead.

I knew I should have tried to make small talk with this man who was being very kind to take even more time out of his already blown-out-of-the-water schedule. But I couldn't think of a thing to say.

I clutched the armrest on the door and tried to calm myself down. Of course, Buddy would be fine. My reaction was totally over the top.

With nothing better to do, I tried to apply my knowledge of psychology to analyzing said reaction. I have a masters degree in it, but I hadn't done much with it, other than teach a few college courses part-time. And use what I knew about behavior modification to train my dogs.

Best I could figure I was diverting my anxiety and upset over the old lady's death into worry about Buddy.

I stared at the fingernails of my left hand, cut down to the quick by a CSI technician over an evidence bag. There were still tiny reddish-brown crescents under the edge of two of them.

I decided I had a right to be irrational. It wasn't every day that someone practically died in your arms.

CHAPTER SEVEN

Of course, Buddy and Felix were both fine. Larry—he'd insisted I call him that—had loaded them into the back of his SUV and chauffeured us all back to my car at the shopping center lot.

However, one could not say that the Blacks' house was fine. This time the cops hadn't been nearly so careful.

The contents of my duffle bag were strewn across the bed, which had been stripped of its bedding. The sheets and comforter were a tangled mess on the floor. And not only had Buddy's food been dumped again, this time about half of it had been crunched under foot as someone had stood at the bathroom vanity and searched the medicine cabinet, depositing my toiletries—the only thing I'd gotten around to unpacking—into the sink.

My phone rang in my pocket as I stood in the doorway, staring at the mess.

It was Will.

I burst into tears.

"What? What's the matter?" His voice rose in pitch as I continued to sob. "Talk to me, Marcia. Are you okay? Is Buddy… oh, no, something's happened to Buddy."

"No, thank God!" Between sniffles and hiccups, I told him the story. Well, not exactly the *whole* story. There were a few tiny omissions.

By the time I'd finished, he was almost as mad as I had been. I could hear his teeth grinding through the phone. "I'm on my way."

"There isn't much you can do." I was now sitting in the middle of my bed, on top of my crumpled clothes.

"I was coming over anyway, remember?"

"Oh yeah, our night on the beach." Another sob escaped from my throat.

"Maybe we'll do that tomorrow night," Will said. "Tonight I'll help you clean up."

"Okay," I managed to get out. I was blubbering again.

"You gonna be okay?" He sounded worried.

"Yes, now that you're coming."

"I'm already on the road. Be there in an hour."

We signed off, and suddenly I felt motivated to at least put some of the chaos to rights. I hung up my rumpled clothes and remade my bed.

Then I went out into the living room, and almost lost it again.

Poor Felix was wandering around the room, sniffing at dislodged sofa cushions and drawer contents dumped on the floor. He stopped and turned his head toward me, the most sorrowful look in his big eyes.

I went over and sat on the floor next to him. My arm draped over his thick neck, I whispered, "It's okay, boy. They'll be back eventually."

I wondered if it was a sin to lie to a dog.

Will and I sat at the kitchen table, eating the carryout pizza I'd ordered and drinking the bottle of wine Will had brought.

It wasn't exactly the romantic evening either of us had in mind, but I was unwilling to leave Felix, considering his current mopey mood. I'd called the motel while waiting for Will. It had been hard enough to get them to agree to one large dog in the room. Two was a definite no, so I'd cancelled the reservation.

I felt okay with inviting Will to stay here though, since it was unlikely that Jake and Janey would make bail this time.

"How'd you end up at that pawn shop this morning?" Will asked as he selected another slice of pizza.

I was afraid he'd get around to asking that eventually. My

sins of omission during my earlier telling of the tale were about to come back to bite me.

"Well, I was out exploring this morning and I stopped by the sheriff's department…"

Will paused, pizza slice halfway to his mouth.

"And I happened to run into one of the deputies," I continued in what I hoped was an innocent-sounding voice, "a sergeant actually, who happened to be here Friday, so I asked him what was happening on the case."

The pizza slice still dangled over Will's plate. He arched an eyebrow at me.

"Um, and he suggested I talk to this guy, Larry Merrick, who's a biker."

Will put the pizza down on his plate. "Why exactly would this sergeant suggest that?" His tone implied that he wasn't buying my I-just-happened-to-stop-there approach. Sheriff departments weren't normally on the list of tourist attractions.

"He was acting kind of funny, like he was trying to tell me, between the lines, that his department wasn't looking at any other possibilities other than Jake and Janey."

"And why exactly would that have anything to do with you?" He finally picked up the pizza and took a bite.

Was that a smile he was trying to hide as he chewed?

Okay, that ticked me off. He was playing with me.

"Look, I care about these people, and I know it is physically impossible for Jake to be the guy who robbed the pawn shop Thursday."

"Because you think he can't ride on two wheels anymore, but you don't know that for sure."

I glared at him. "Yes, I do know that for sure."

He took another bite of pizza. "So, the sergeant passed you off to this Merrick guy. And?"

"And he suggested I meet him at the pawn shop and he'd introduce me to the owners and then we'd go… um, talk about the biking scene here."

"Was he there when you got there?"

I shook my head. "I went into the shop and then I heard moaning, and found the lady…" I stopped, not really willing to relive those moments yet again.

"Hey," I said, "I need to find out what's going on with their case now, you know, so I know what to do about Felix. Do you think you could go with me tomorrow to the sheriff's department and maybe ask, as a professional courtesy…" I trailed off again as Will started chuckling.

"Marcia, you are too much. Do you really think I'm that dumb?"

"Of course I don't think you're dumb. But I do need to find out what I should do with Felix if Jake and Janey are going to be locked up for a while. I can't stay here forever."

"Okay, I'll go with you to talk to this sergeant tomorrow, but only if you promise to drop all this after that, and let the sheriff and his people do their jobs."

"Sure," I said, while crossing my fingers in my lap.

It is definitely a sin to lie to your boyfriend… um, male friend… lover? I never know what to call Will.

"By the way, the Buckland County sheriff is a she."

Will tilted his head to one side but made no comment as he took another bite of pizza.

Despite it being a Sunday, the sheriff was in. We were escorted to her office, where she stood behind a large oak desk, her hand extended.

"Sheriff Haines, a pleasure to meet you in person." She gave Will a big smile but practically ignored me. "I'm a big admirer of yours."

Will looked a bit startled. "Uh, the pleasure's mine." He shook the proffered hand, then pointed in my direction. "This is my, um, friend, Marcia Banks." Will had the same dilemma regarding what thirty-something romantic partners should call each other, but this time I wished he'd opted for girlfriend.

Especially when I caught the glint in the sheriff's eye.

"Please, have a seat." She waved at two visitors' chairs in front of her desk. "I heard about the work you did to root out corruption in Collins County. Impressive."

Will's rugged, tanned cheeks took on a pink tinge. He shrugged, then cleared his throat. "I'm not here in an official capacity of course, but I was hoping you could tell us the status of Jacob Black and his wife."

The sheriff's eyebrows shot up. "They've been arrested for murder, as Ms. Banks should well know, since she's one of our witnesses."

I resisted the urge to shake my head. I wasn't about to testify against Jake and Janey, although I had no idea how I would get out of it.

"Do you think it's likely they will make bail?" Will asked.

"I doubt it, since this new crime was committed while they were out on bail from the first robbery."

"The don't have an alibi?" Will asked.

The sheriff shook her head. "None that can be confirmed. Mr. Black claims he was out on his motorcycle, on country roads, with only his dog as a witness. Mrs. Black says she was grocery shopping, but no one at the store could specifically remember her being there. And she didn't save her receipt."

I leaned forward. "Are you looking at any other possibilities?"

The sheriff turned to face me, her eyes hard. "No. We're not in the habit of arresting people unless we're pretty darn sure they're the culprits."

"But I know Jake couldn't have done this," I blurted out.

The sheriff took a deep breath, then let it out in what sounded an awful lot like a long-suffering sigh. "I appreciate your loyalty to your friends, but you yourself have put them on the scene. You saw them in their truck."

"No," I said, my voice terse, "I saw a truck the same color as theirs, and half the other pickups in this state. And the two people in it, I can hardly identify them, can I? Since I didn't see their faces."

Will held up his hand in a stop gesture. "What has Ms. Banks most concerned is that she believes Mr. Black is physically incapable of riding a two-wheeled motorcycle, because of his balance problems due to his head injury."

"I *believe*," the sheriff said, her own tone tart, "that Lieutenant Harrison has him scheduled for a complete neurological exam at Daytona General Hospital tomorrow."

A snort got out before I could catch it. Will shot me a warning glance.

I resisted the urge to shake my head. Daytona General had one of the worst reputations in the State of Florida.

The sheriff glared at me. The furrow between her eyes had turned into a trench. "Mr. Black can have his own doctors testify at the trial, but we will use whomever we deem appropriate to do our evaluation."

I stifled another snort. "Is S–"

"Thanks so much for your time, Sheriff." Will stood abruptly. "We can find our way out."

He grabbed my arm and pulled me to a stand.

I let him drag me from the sheriff's office, but once her door was closed, I pulled loose. "What are you doing?"

"Keeping you from getting your sergeant friend in hot water."

"Oh." I deflated. He had a point. Asking for Sergeant Phelps right after we had locked horns over the neurological evaluation would have likely put the man in an awkward spot.

We inquired about Phelps at the front reception window and were told he wasn't on duty today.

"Now what?" I said, once we were out on the hot sidewalk.

Will huffed out air and shook his head. "I might have gotten more out of the sheriff if you hadn't gotten her back up."

I opened my mouth to protest, then clamped it shut again. "Sorry," I muttered.

He put his hands on my shoulders. "Look, you've got a few more days before you can get back into your house, so just stay at Jake's with Felix and see what happens. The docs at Daytona may very well determine that it couldn't have been him on the motorcycle that first time, and they'll let them go."

I sighed. "I guess."

"Hey, you promised you'd leave it alone if I came with you today."

I didn't say anything.

"Marcia?" Will's tone had a sharp edge.

"I've been thinking about a comment Becky made, that maybe Sergeant Phelps encouraged me to get involved because there was something rotten going on in the sheriff's department."

Will's eyes had narrowed but he didn't interrupt me.

"Is there any way to check these people out?"

Shaking his head, Will dropped his hands from my shoulders and turned toward his car. I followed him across the parking lot.

Once in his car, he said, "You mean the people in the sheriff's department here?"

"Yeah, the ones on Jake and Janey's case at least, and maybe the sheriff." I held my breath.

He stared straight ahead for several seconds. Then he sighed. He seemed to be doing that a lot lately. "I guess it can't hurt to run background checks on them. Make me a list of their names."

He turned in his seat and crooked a finger under my chin, lifting my face and forcing me to meet his eyes. "Then you're going to let it go, right?"

"Sure," I said out loud, even as I was plotting how I would track down Sergeant Phelps tomorrow.

I obviously wasn't destined to get a full night's sleep. My phone rang at seven, when I had only just drifted back into a sound slumber, after Will had left at six to drive back to Collinsville.

We'd never made it to the beach last night either. I'd been reluctant to leave a still mopey Felix alone for the night.

My phone insistently buzzed again. I felt around on the nightstand without opening my eyes and finally connected with the plastic rectangle.

"Hello," I mumbled, then realized I was talking to the back of the phone.

When I turned it around, I discovered that my neighbor Edna was in mid-conversation. She doesn't always require a partner in such endeavors.

"…ain't too impressed with what they're doin' over there," she was saying when my brain finally engaged.

"What? Edna, start over."

"Yer contractor seems to be a tad flustered. He's runnin' 'round like a chicken with his head chopped off."

"Wha'?" I sat up in bed. Buddy, lying on the rug on one side, jumped up and put his head up on the edge of the comforter. Felix, on the other side, rose more slowly and stretched his bulky body.

"I think there's somethin' wrong," Edna said. "You want I should send Dexter over to find out what?"

"No, no." I could only begin to imagine what twisted tale I'd get from Dexter. "Let me call the contractor. I'll get back to you."

I disconnected and then called Pete Jennings, the contractor Will had found for me through a friend on the Ocala police force.

"Hey, Pete. Good morning," I faked a cheerfulness I sure as heck wasn't feeling. "How are things going?"

"Um, too early to tell yet, Marcia. I'm still assessing the extent of the damage."

I let a beat of silence go by. "I thought you'd done that before, when you gave me a quote."

"Um, that was an estimate, and it's lookin' like the termites got into more of the roof than I'd originally thought."

Dread lay like a brick in my stomach. "What do you mean?"

"We may have to replace more of the rafters and, um, about half of the roof itself."

My stomach threatened to toss the brick across the room. "How much?"

"Uh, don't know yet. I'll have to call you back in a bit. My guys are still up there, assessing the damage." He disconnected.

Why aren't you up there?

A jumble of emotions roiled in my stomach—anxiety, confusion, frustration. I grabbed ahold of the latter and let it blossom into full-blown anger in my chest, as I punched Will's speed dial number.

"Good morning, Sunshine," he sang cheerfully. The sound of road noise said he was still *en route* to Collinsville.

"Sunshine, schmunshine. That jerk you recommended is trying to rip me off."

"Pete? I didn't recommend him, my buddy on the Ocala PD did."

I filled Will in on my conversations with Edna and Pete.

"Lemme swing by and see what's up," he said. "It's not that far out of the way."

Actually, it was, but I didn't argue. "Thanks. Sorry I snapped at you."

"S'okay. I'm a grouch too when I get yanked out a sound sleep by bad news. I'll call you back after I talk to Pete."

"Let me know if I need to get over there and supervise things personally."

There, that sounded like I was in control… which obviously I was not.

Unwilling to just sit around and worry, I loaded the dogs in the car and we took a ride to Buckland Beach. I'd seen a sign somewhere in my travels that said dogs were prohibited on the beach June through August. I took that to mean they were allowed in September.

Buckland Beach was only a few miles long—sandwiched between Ormond Beach to the north and Daytona to the south—but it was beautiful. It reminded me of Crescent Beach further up the coast, with mainly private homes skirting the inland edge of the sandy strip. Most of them were relatively modest—a working-class Crescent Beach then—but a few were huge, with big glass walls looking out at the sparkling ocean.

If I were naturally an envious person, these would be the

houses I'd envy more than Jake and Janey's place. "Wouldn't it be great to the live on the beach?" I asked the dogs. Felix rolled an eye in my direction. Buddy cocked his head.

Crossing my wrists in front of me, then spreading them apart again, I gave them the release signal just to be clear that this was play time.

Buddy romped along the edge of the small waves, chasing and nipping at the white foam. Felix stayed closer to my side, eyeing the ebbing and flowing water with suspicion.

I scanned the beach ahead of us. We were pretty much alone, only a few people at some distance, and they were walking away from us.

I turned Buddy loose and found a stick to throw. He chased it and brought it back several times. Felix stirred beside me and looked up with his typical baleful expression.

"Okay, boy." I called Buddy to me and put him back on his leash. He flopped down on the sand, panting. Then I let Felix go and threw the stick for him. He trotted after it, in no apparent hurry.

"Fancy meeting you here." A deep, breathy voice from behind me.

CHAPTER EIGHT

I jumped and whirled around. Buddy was on his feet, inserting himself between me and the stranger.

Except he wasn't a stranger. Larry Merrick, in running shorts and a tank top, jogged in place a few feet away. "Sorry, didn't mean to startle you. Have you recovered from your ordeal yesterday?"

An involuntary shudder at the memory gave him his answer.

"Sorry again, I shouldn't have brought it up."

Felix had just now reached the stick and turned to trot back with it. I headed in his direction. Larry fell into step beside me.

"You come here often?" I asked.

"Yes, it's one of my favorite stretches of beach. I run here every chance I get."

We intercepted Felix. The stick was slimy with his slobber. I threw it one more time for him, then put him back on his leash.

Larry was still strolling along with us, apparently willing to interrupt his run.

I was acutely aware of how good-looking he was, something that had barely registered the other two times I'd seen him, when I'd been more than a little distracted by other things.

Neatly trimmed black hair framed his tanned, boyish face. Muscular arms and legs suggested that he did indeed run here regularly. His brown eyes sparkled, as if he knew a joke that nobody else was in on.

"How's Mr. Belenky taking his wife's death?" I asked.

"Not well." Larry frowned and kicked sand with the toe of his running shoe. "I'm going with Izzy later to talk to the sheriff's people. He was too upset yesterday to be interviewed."

"Izzy?"

"Isaiah."

"Um, I'd intended the other day to ask you to introduce me to some of the motorcycle gangs in the area…" Now I was wondering if that was such a great idea, after the attack on Mrs. Belenky.

"Clubs," Larry said.

"Wha? They attacked her with clubs?"

"No, no." He gave me a small smile. "Motorcycle clubs, not gangs."

"Oh, sorry," snarky Marcia snuck past my guard, "didn't mean to not be PC."

"It's not about being politically correct. The bikers in *clubs* come from all walks of life, and many are middle class like me and the Blacks. The purpose of the clubs is to organize rides and other events related to our common interest." He was beginning to sound like the lawyer that he was, giving a summation to a jury. "The *gangs* are the outlaw bikers."

"Oh." I felt vaguely ashamed for lumping all bikers together, especially since I knew Jake and Janey were good people.

And why was snarky Marcia so on edge today?

Duh! Finding a dying woman, she informed me.

I silently conceded that she had a point.

"So it probably is a gang member who is doing this, versus a club member?"

Larry blew out air. "Yeah."

We'd reached the end of Buckland Beach and a sign that prohibited dogs completely from Ormond Beach. I wheeled around as smoothly as one can with two large dogs in tow. Larry stepped aside to give us room, then we started back the other way.

"I know a guy who straddles the fence. A few bikers do. I could take you to talk to Jojo. He might know something."

"That would be great." I gave him a big smile to show my appreciation.

He smiled back. "It'll have to be later this afternoon. I'll pick you up at, say four?"

"Great. You know where Jake's house is?"

"Yeah, I've been there." Then he seemed to hesitate. "It's on 127th Street, right?"

I nodded.

"They had a big party there about a year ago, invited a bunch of bikers." He peeled away from us as we neared the spot where he'd first joined us. "See you later," he called back over his shoulder as he jogged off down the beach.

I waved and headed for the car with two tired, sandy but happy dogs.

My phone rang as I was driving back to Jake and Janey's.

Will flashed on the Bluetooth screen.

"Hey," I said.

"It's not as bad as Pete made it sound," he jumped in without preamble. "The termites got into the front soffit and one of the boards of the roof itself is rotted. Looks like there was a leak at some point and the previous owner repaired the shingles but not the board underneath."

"What's a soffit?" I asked, glad I didn't have to expose my ignorance of such things to Pete.

"That wooden strip under the edge of the roof. He's replacing it with aluminum. One less thing to rot in the future."

I braced myself as I turned into Jake's driveway. "How much?"

"Shouldn't be more than a couple hundred more."

I took that news with mixed emotions. It wasn't as bad as I'd feared, but even a couple of hundred was more than I had. Will had offered to float me a loan if need be, but I wasn't willing to go there yet.

"Okay, thanks for checking on it for me."

"No problem. Hey, can we meet somewhere halfway for dinner tonight?"

My heart felt heavy in my chest. Apparently, he'd given up on the plan to have an evening in a beach motel. I could hardly blame him. Who knew what would happen or who would get themselves killed to thwart that plan again?

"What's halfway in between?" I asked.

"Not sure. I'll look on a map and get back to you."

"Okay, talk to you later."

I now had several hours to kill before meeting Larry to go to this Jojo's place. I took the dogs around back and wiped their paws before letting them inside. Then I made sure they had plenty of fresh water.

After some thought, I decided to write two notes and tape them to the outsides of the doors.

Note to Police or Other Officials:

I am in residence here and am taking full responsibility for Jacob Black's service dog. If you remove either him or my dog from these premises again, you will be facing a lawsuit.

Marcia Banks

I then took a picture of each note with my phone before getting back in my car.

Okay, maybe I was being paranoid but I was getting really tired of going to Animal Services every other day.

At the sheriff's department, I sat in a far corner of the waiting area, trying to be as invisible as possible in case the lady sheriff came out. The deputy at the receptionist window, a male one this time, had said Sergeant Phelps was tied up but would probably be able to see me soon.

The door to the inner sanctum opened and I sat up a bit straighter, hoping it was the sergeant, fearing it was the sheriff.

Instead, a roly-poly man with gray tufts of hair around a bald pate came through it. Larry Merrick followed close behind, now in a business suit.

Larry spotted me and whispered something in the older man's ear.

The man looked in my direction, then raced over, moving a lot faster than his girth implied was possible. "Ms. Banks, oh my," he was half spluttering, half crying, "you were the one who found my Elsie. My poor, poor Elsie." This came out on a wail.

He stopped and seemed to visibly gather himself. "I'm sorry, but I need to know. Did my Elsie suffer? They were saying something about her back. Did the man who did this, did he hurt her bad?"

I found myself standing, my mouth hanging open.

Of course he hurt her bad. He killed her. I clamped my mouth shut so those words couldn't accidentally fall out.

But I'm a crappy liar. The best I could come up with was, "I don't think she was in a lot of pain." Then I quickly added, "Did she have back problems?"

Izzy shook his head. "She was in good shape, for her age."

Which had to be seventy if it was a day, so, yes, she probably had the occasional back ache. But I doubted she would've wasted her dying breath on complaints about an achy back. In my heart of hearts, I knew darn well she'd said, "Jake Black."

But that didn't mean someone wasn't impersonating Jake. Obviously, the true culprit was trying to frame him.

"Did they take much from your store?" I asked, at a loss for what else to say.

Izzy nodded. "They got the diamonds." Then he collapsed into himself, his head in his hands, crying. "And they killed my Elsie."

Larry patted Izzy's shoulder, then whispered, "See you soon," over his crouched back.

My throat tightened and my eyes stung, as I watched him escort the heartbroken old man out of the sheriff's department's front door.

"Ms. Banks," the deputy at the reception window called over. "Sergeant Phelps is still tied up. He said he'd call you later."

"Thank you." I headed for the door.

I was no sooner outside on the sidewalk than my phone rang. The number was unfamiliar but it was a 386 area code, the one for this part of the state.

"Stop coming around the department," a male voice said as soon as I'd picked up. He sounded a little angry.

"Sergeant?"

"Yeah. Look, I can't help you anymore. You've gotta talk to the bikers."

"I'm trying to do that, but I need to know what's going on in the investigation. The sheriff said that you all aren't looking into anybody else."

"Nope, especially after the eval we got this morning."

"Eval? You mean the neurological evaluation on Jake? What were the results?"

"I can't tell you." He cleared his throat. "But Jake can. Visiting hours are four to eight tonight. I'll make sure you're on his list."

"Thanks, but…" The sergeant had disconnected.

The garage that Larry and I entered a few minutes after four that afternoon had nothing in common with Jake Black's except for the presence of motorcycles.

Two bare lightbulbs hanging from rafters cast macabre shadows in the corners of one of the dirtiest spaces under roof that I'd ever seen. The only things that were clean were the two motorcycles in the middle of the floor. They were pristine.

The garage owner, Joseph Johnson, aka Jojo, was a study in what would happen if you crossed a bear with a Hell's Angel. He wasn't particularly tall—six feet, maybe an inch more—but he probably weighed over two-fifty. About half of that weight was in muscular arms, legs and a barrel-shaped, hairy chest. The other half was from a huge beer belly that defied his leather vest's efforts to cover it. His jeans were more grease-colored than blue, and an equally greasy red bandana held back longish, shaggy gray hair. But the eyes that looked out from between gray, bushy brows and leathery, stubbled cheeks were the clearest blue I'd ever seen.

"Do you know Jake well?" I asked.

"Sure," Jojo said around a lump of something I really didn't want to think about. "Him and me, we're buddies. We're in the Moto Guzzi club over in Daytona, 'long with Bach here." He gestured toward Larry.

I raised an eyebrow in the lawyer's direction. "Motogoochie? What's that?"

Larry had shucked his suit coat and his tie, but he still looked seriously out of place in this dingy garage. He pointed to one of the motorcycles, a sleek machine, with red and cream-colored fenders. "It's a brand of bike, Italian. I've got one, and so does Jake."

"His dark blue one?" I asked.

Larry nodded.

I walked around Jojo's other motorcycle, which was all black. "This looks like Jake's other bike."

"Naw, that's a Harley," Jojo said. "Jake's got an Indian."

I resisted the urge to roll my eyes. All these brands and such were making me a little crazy. "What's the difference?"

Larry laughed. "Watch who you say that in front of. Harley owners are very loyal. They don't like having their bikes compared to others, unless it's to say they're a whole lot better."

"Aw, I don't know," Jojo said. "I don't mind it bein' compared to an Indian. They were some amazing bikes."

"Were?" I said.

"They stopped making Indians in the 1950's," Larry said. "But a new company bought them and started production again in the 90's. Jake got one of the original ones and rebuilt it."

"Main difference in the looks is in the fenders." Jojo tapped said fender of his Harley. "Indian bikes got real distinct-lookin' ones that come down on the sides."

Now that he mentioned it, I remembered that Jake's bike had more elaborate fenders than this one.

"Jojo," I said, "I need your help. You know about Jake and Janey's troubles, right?"

He tilted his head in a slight nod, his expression a tad wary.

"I don't think the sheriff's department is investigating any other suspects." Actually, I *knew* this, didn't just think it. But I didn't want to sound like I was dissing the county sheriff, even though I seriously wanted to. "So I need to try to find out who else might drive bikes like Jake's and Janey's."

Jojo cringed. "Ride, not *drive*. An' who'd ya have in mind?"

"I don't know, but I was wondering if you know any of the, um, less law-abiding bikers in town."

Jojo stared at me for a long moment. "Might know some, but none of 'em rides an Indian, and even their ole ladies wouldn't be caught dead on no Goldwing trike like Janey's."

"Could you keep your eyes and ears open?" Larry said. "Maybe somebody new has joined the group."

Jojo tilted his head to one side, then nodded it once. "Sure, Bach. For Jake."

"Thanks." Larry extended a hand, which Jojo shook with one of his big, greasy paws. I could tell Larry was struggling to hide a frown. Jojo and I exchanged cell phone numbers and goodbyes.

Once safely ensconced in Larry's SUV, I asked, "What group did you mean?"

"The Florida Dark Demons," he said as he wiped grease off his hand with a rag he'd retrieved from the back floor. "They're a true biker gang, although they put up a mild pretense that they're a regular club. But they're definitely one percenters."

"What's that mean? That they're rich?"

Larry snorted as he started the engine. "Hardly. One percenter refers to the degree to which they participate in society, or the degree to which they obey the law and the rules of social etiquette. They do both as little as they can get away with."

"I guess you don't call them one percenters to their faces though."

He snorted again as he backed out of Jojo's dirt driveway. "They call themselves that. They're proud of it. I think the Dark Demons have a website. Check them out, but whatever you do, don't engage with them, online or in person."

"And Jojo's a member?"

He nodded. "On the periphery. Sorry he couldn't help more,

but he'll probably nose around some. He does like Jake."

"I appreciate you taking me to meet him."

"Happy to help. I like Jake too."

"What was it Jojo called you? Bok, as in bok choy?"

Larry chuckled. "No. Bach, as in the composer. I listen to classical music when I'm riding."

"Why do some bikers have more than one bike?" I asked as he pulled out onto A1A.

"They serve different purposes. Jojo's Moto Guzzi is their sports model. It's streamlined and fast, but not very comfortable on long rides. His Harley is their cruising bike, bigger and heavier with a broader seat."

"Doesn't Harley make fast bikes?"

Larry glanced at me and grinned. "That's like asking if Santa's elves make toys? Harley owners will claim their bikes are the fastest, even the big cruising bikes."

"I thought you said Harley owners are loyal to the brand. So why does Jojo have a Moto Guzzi?"

"He had it first. Then he bought a Harley when he started hanging around with some of the Demons."

"Why is he doing that? He seems like a nice guy."

"He is, but he's retired and widowed, and kind of at loose ends. I think he's reliving his adolescence, trying to be the rebel he was too responsible to be back then."

A warmth spread in my chest. I liked this guy. He was very astute.

I opened my mouth to ask another question, but my phone chose that moment to ring.

It was Will.

"Hey," I said into the phone.

"Hey yourself." He sounded cheery. "How about dinner in Winter Park? There's an Italian place not far from I-4. It's about an hour from you. They've got a patio, so you can bring Buddy."

"Um, I've got something I need to do first. It'll be another hour, maybe a bit more, before I can head your way."

"What do you need to do?" he asked.

I bristled a little, then realized that was my own guilt reaction. It was an innocent question from his perspective.

"Uh, I'll tell you about it when I see you. Is seven-thirty too late for you?"

"Nope. Should have cooled down some by then."

I seriously doubted that, but I appreciated his willingness to endure some heat and humidity for Buddy's sake.

"I'll make a reservation." Will gave me the address of the restaurant. "See you then."

When I'd lowered my phone to my lap, Larry said, "Guess that answers my question."

"What?"

"I was going to ask you to have dinner with me."

My cheeks warmed. "Uh... sorry, I'm involved."

"I gathered. My bad luck." He flashed me another grin before returning his gaze to the road. "Let me know, if you become uninvolved."

"Uh..." I seemed to be saying that a lot lately, "I'm flattered though. You know, that you're, um, interested." I clamped my mouth shut before I dug myself deeper into a hole.

We rode in semi-awkward silence for the last few blocks. At Jake and Janey's, Larry offered to walk me to the door.

"No need," I quickly said and jumped out. I stuck my head back inside the SUV. "Thanks for your help."

After a quick check on the dogs, I was in my own car and back on the road, headed for the sheriff's department again.

Only this time I went into the back entrance, through the door marked *Buckland County Jail.*

I was prepared for an orange jumpsuit, the color my other incarcerated client had worn. Instead, Jake was dressed in a light beige shirt and elastic-waist pants with no pockets.

And I didn't have to visit him in his cell. He was escorted by a deputy to the other side of a glass barrier, which I suspected was bulletproof.

We both picked up phone receivers. They were so much more high tech on the coast than in rural central Florida.

"How's Felix?" Jake asked.

"He's fine. A bit mopey. He misses you."

He swallowed hard. "And Janey?"

"I don't know. I'll try to see her tomorrow."

He nodded. "Our lawyer says she's holding up okay, but…"

My chest ached. "Are you happy with your lawyer?" I asked, more to change the subject than anything else. I was kind of wondering why he hadn't called on Larry Merrick to represent him. Then again, maybe that would have been a conflict of interest since Larry was representing Izzy Belenky.

"Yeah, he's good. One of the best in the area for criminal law." Jake seemed distracted.

"What were the results of the neurological evaluation this morning?" I blurted out. I wasn't sure how much time we had and I needed to get as much information from him as possible.

He looked a little startled by the abrupt change of subject, then he gathered himself. "The doc agreed with me that it's hard to prove a negative. His report said, quote, 'inconclusive regarding balance issues.'"

Anger flared in my chest. Apparently, the sheriff was more than ready to interpret 'inconclusive' as no balance problems.

Reining in my emotions, I asked, "Do you know anybody else in the area who rides an Indian bike?"

He actually grinned at me. "You've been doing your homework."

I gave him a small smile.

"No," he said. "They're not real common. I don't know anybody else in Buckland County who has one, although I've seen some around Daytona Beach."

"During Bike Week?"

He let out a clipped chuckle. "No. There I've seen plenty of pretty much every bike made. Bikers come from all over the country to Daytona for Bike Week." He narrowed his eyes at me. "What are you up to, Marcia?"

"I've just been trying to sort out the biker scene here, to see if I can find out who else might have done this."

He pursed his lips and furrowed his brow. "That could be dangerous. Not all bikers are law-abiding citizens."

"So I've discovered." Actually, I'd been more surprised that most of them were. But the few that weren't, they were a different story. "What do you know about the Florida Dark Demons?"

Jake's face blanched. His knuckles clutching the phone receiver turned white. "Dear God, Marcia, stay away from them."

I took a deep breath. "I can't, Jake. They may be the answer to who is really doing this."

"Marcia…" His voice was tight, his eyes dark with despair. I suspected he wanted to warn me off, but at the same time desperately hoped I'd keep seeking that answer.

Something solidified inside of me. I'd had one client commit suicide while in jail for a crime he didn't commit. I wasn't going to let it happen again.

He cleared his throat, sat up straighter, obviously pulling himself together. "You're in over your head."

"Probably. But I'm not going to let you and Janey go to prison for something you didn't do."

I must have sounded convincing because he sucked in air, then blew it out. "The Demons. It probably was them doing all this. I got the impression that some valuable stuff was taken."

I filed that tidbit away. "I already talked to Jojo Johnson."

He grimaced. "You see his shop?"

I grinned, determined to lighten the mood. "Yeah. Bet it makes you hyperventilate."

He let out a short bark of laughter. Then his face sobered. "Be careful, Marcia."

CHAPTER NINE

Another quick stop at the house. I'd checked Felix's water bowl, changed my clothes, and was about to leave for Winter Park, when my phone rang.

Mattie flashed up on caller ID. The director of the agency I train for tends to keep conversations short, so I answered.

"Hey there," I said cheerfully.

"We've got a problem," Mattie replied in her no-nonsense style. "Our accountant is having a cow because we sold Buddy to you."

"What?"

"He says it could cost us our not-for-profit status."

I staggered to the nearest armchair in the Blacks' living room. Falling into it, I said, "What are we going to do?"

"Don't know. There's a lawyer on our board of directors. I've got a call in to him. But tax law is complicated. He may not know enough about it to help us."

Panic jumbled my brain. Suddenly Felix was beside me, leaning his bulk against my legs. He wasn't "on duty" but he'd apparently sensed my anxiety and was doing what now came naturally to him.

I absently stroked the soft fur on his head and scratched his ears.

Buddy sat several feet away, his head cocked in his what's-up look.

My chest hurt so bad I thought I might be having a heart

attack. One thing I knew, I wasn't giving him back to the agency.

"I'll let you know what I find out." And Mattie was gone.

I stared at my phone, feeling like someone had hollowed out my insides.

Seriously? What else can go wrong in my life?

Don't answer that, Lord!

The last thing I wanted to do right now was eat, but Will would already be on his way to the restaurant. I didn't have the heart to call him and tell him to turn around.

With effort, I drummed up the energy to stand up. I said good-bye to Felix, and Buddy and I headed out.

I was still ruminating over Mattie's call when I pulled into the restaurant's parking lot fifty minutes later. Surely there had to be an answer that didn't involve my losing Buddy, but my gut suspicion was that there wasn't. To accountants and lawyers and IRS employees, Buddy was an "asset" that belonged to the agency, one they could give to a deserving veteran but not to me.

All those accountants and lawyers and such would say, "Just train another mentor dog." They wouldn't get it that Buddy was like my child. He wasn't interchangeable with another dog.

I looked up at the one-story tan building, nestled amongst a stand of live oaks and palm trees. A bright red sign announced the name—*Giovanni's*—a drawing of a chubby dude in a chef's cap beside the tall letters.

Normally, I would find the place charming, but tonight my stomach clenched at the thought of food.

Will was already seated on the screened porch behind the restaurant. I apologized for being late, but he brushed it off. "I've only been here a few minutes."

I opened my mouth to tell him why I'd been delayed but a waiter appeared and asked about drinks.

I threw caution to the wind and asked for a glass of white wine. Then I sat down and gestured for Buddy to lie at my feet.

"Coffee," Will said, then turned to me. "I'm starved. Let's go ahead and order. They've got shrimp Alfredo."

"That's fine," I muttered. Normally shrimp Alfredo is a favorite, but tonight I doubted I'd be able to choke much down.

He gave me a funny look as he ordered that for me and spaghetti and meatballs for himself.

As soon as the waiter had left, he said, "Marcia, we really need to consider all this."

I stared at him. "All what?"

"The whole distance thing."

My mind was still miles away, worrying about Buddy. "What do you mean?"

He leaned forward across the table, grabbed my hand in his. "All this stuff that your house needs, maybe it's a sign of some kind?"

I narrowed my eyes. "A sign?"

"You know, a sign from God or something." He gave me a sappy smile.

Seriously? Did he think because I was a preacher's kid that invoking a sign from God was going to get me to comply with whatever he had in mind?

He had the good sense to adjust to my mood. His face sobered. "I've been thinking. If I sold my place, I could pay for the repairs to your house and then some. Build an extension—a study for me, and a big deck, maybe a sunroom."

Crapola. The dang termites had given him the perfect opening.

I opted to stall. "Let's see what happens when I get the final bill." Too late I realized how mercenary that sounded—as if I'd consider taking his contribution if the costs were too high. "I didn't mean that the way it came out."

He squeezed my hand. "Sweetheart, I get it that you're gun-shy, but how long are we gonna drag this out?"

To infinity, my snarky self retorted internally.

Why was I so resistant to living together? It certainly wasn't because I lacked an attraction to Will's body. Indeed, the thought of going to bed with this man every night of my life made my heart go ballistic in my chest.

And I had to admit that it wasn't about trust either. I knew he loved me and that he was a good guy. He would never intentionally hurt me.

The invisible issue between us raised its ugly head. If we moved in together that brought us one step closer to…

He sighed and sat back in his chair, letting go of my hand, as the waiter arrived with our drinks and salads. A busboy followed him, carrying a dish with water in it for Buddy.

The simple, kind gesture almost made me cry. But I was so near the edge, probably just about anything would have made me cry right then. This was so not the night to be having this discussion.

Will waited until they had left. "Why are you so freaked by the idea of having kids?"

I took a large swig of wine without answering him. I didn't *have* an answer for him, and he knew it. My counselor, Jo Ann had asked me the same question, a couple of times. I'd evaded it. Now I was kind of glad for the financially imposed hiatus from counseling.

So of course, my fickle mind decided to chew on the question now. I guess it was desperate for a distraction.

I flashed suddenly to a girl I'd gone to elementary school with. She was always a bit disheveled, her clothes wrinkled, her hair a mess. I'd overheard my parents talking about her one day. My mother had said something about the girl's mom being too lazy to get up and see the girl off to school in the morning. "If a person's not going to be responsible for the children she brings into this world, she shouldn't have them," Mom had pronounced to my father.

Did I think I was too irresponsible?

I realized Will was talking and forced my mind back to the here and now.

"All this commuting is getting old," he muttered as he stabbed a cherry tomato in his salad. He popped it into his mouth.

My heart turned to lead and plummeted to my stomach. Was he breaking up with me?

He glanced up and abruptly stopped chewing. Dropping his fork, he reached over and grabbed my hand. "I'm not tired of you, just of dragging halfway across the state to see you. We need to get ourselves into the same town. Or county, at least."

I dropped my gaze to my plate. He was right, and if I wasn't willing to live together than something else had to happen. My job was portable. Although I needed a decent-sized, fenced yard, I could pretty much train dogs anywhere. While his job was in Collins County.

But I loved my little cottage, and my quirky little town. And my feelings about Collinsville were not so positive. That town was full of reminders of unpleasant events.

The waiter was back with our food, and I hadn't touched the salad yet.

Once he was gone, I said, "Let me get past this roof project and then we'll… um, consider options. I can't sell my place with rotted rafters anyway."

Will's eyes widened. "You'd consider selling your place?"

I sucked in air, blew it out slowly. "I'll consider it. Not saying I'll do it, but I'll consider it."

He nodded but he didn't look as happy about my concession as I thought he would. Indeed, as I thought he should.

Then again, I admitted to myself, as concessions went, it was minuscule. Pathetic, even.

Buddy stirred and lapped water from the bowl without getting up. The soft lapping noises blended with the gentle sounds of the surrounding woods settling down for the night. Small creatures rustled in the trees and underbrush. A frog croaked a couple of times, then fell silent.

Again, I thought about how much I'd be enjoying all this if I hadn't picked up that call from Mattie.

I put down my fork. Taking a deep breath, I told Will about the call.

His mouth fell open. "Dear God, could they take Buddy?"

"They can try." My vehemence surprised me. "I'll move across the country and change my name before I let that happen."

"Whoa. I don't think you have to get that drastic." He tried for a chuckle but it sounded half-hearted. The worry in his eyes warmed my chest, even as my stomach clenched even tighter.

"Mattie's going to talk to a lawyer whose on the board."

Will covered my hand with his. "There's no point in worrying about it then," he said in a gentle voice, "until you know more."

I nodded and changed the subject. "When I talked to Becky, it sounded like she and Andy were having a great time."

Will patted my hand and then picked up his fork. "I'm glad to see Andy settled. He's a good man. But who'd have thought Becky…" He trailed off and this time his chuckle was genuine.

I managed a grin and asked him how things were going with his reelection campaign. He said fine. And then he surprised me by asking about the Blacks' case. "Any new developments?"

"The neurological evaluation was, quote, 'inconclusive.' And Sergeant Phelps confirmed they aren't investigating any other suspects."

"That's the way it works, Marcia. Once you've got a suspect and a good case against them, you stop looking. There are too many other demands on a department's resources these days."

"So innocent people get screwed." I didn't mean it to sound as bitter as it came out.

"Sometimes, but their defense attorney will hire a P.I. who'll look for loopholes in the evidence." Will's tone was conciliatory. He was trying to make me feel better, or at least calm me down.

It wasn't working. "All that's going to cost Jake a fortune, and he won't get that money back when he's proven innocent."

Will sighed. "It isn't a perfect system, but it's all we've got. We can't just let criminals go free, but the net's going to sometimes catch some innocents as well."

My phone rang. I quickly silenced it, shooting apologetic looks at the few other diners on the patio.

No name and I didn't recognize the number. I let it go to voicemail.

I chewed on a shrimp. It was all I could do to swallow it. "Did you have time to do those background checks today?"

Will sighed again and put his fork down. He pulled a couple of sheets of folded paper out of his shirt pocket and opened them. "Lieutenant Harrison is a transplant from Maine. His record's clean. A good solid police officer who apparently didn't like the cold North. Phelps and the sheriff are both locals, born and raised in Buckland County. No black marks on their records. Detective Wright's a different story." He grabbed his fork and took a bite of spaghetti.

I was now on the edge of my seat, literally. Pushing my plate slightly away, I leaned on the table. "Come on. Don't drag out the suspense."

Will hastily swallowed. "He was a cop in Newark, New Jersey, until three years ago. There were rumors of corruption, taking pay-offs, serious enough that he was put on desk duty while they were investigated. But he quietly resigned and then showed up down here, with a good recommendation from his immediate superior."

"Is there any way to find out more about the stuff he was doing?"

"Allegedly doing and probably not officially, but I know someone on the Newark force. I'll make a call tomorrow." He ate another quick bite of spaghetti. "Which reminds me, I called a couple of the sheriffs in the counties surrounding Buckland. Figured they'd know Tabitha Baker. I mentioned I'd just met her in person and got them talking some."

He paused to stuff a meatball in his mouth.

"And?" I said, resisting the urge to wrestle his fork away from him.

"They had nothing but good things to say about her."

I slumped back in my chair. Why did I have it in for the lady sheriff?

Uh, because she gushed all over your man, snarky me said inside.

"Aren't you hungry?" Will pointed at my almost full plate with his fork, another meatball jammed on its tines.

"No, not very." I'd been starving before the call from Mattie. I pushed that thought aside.

"Marcia," Will's voice was gentle, "you need to consider the possibility that Jake did this."

I knew he was only trying to prepare me, in case the Blacks were found guilty. But I shook my head. "Maybe he'd steal, although I find that hard to believe, but Jake Black would never, ever hit an old lady on the head. He's kinda old school when it comes to women."

We fell silent as Will ate and I pretended to. The waiter came, tsked at me and then disappeared to find a box.

Will walked us to my car in the restaurant's parking lot. With Buddy waiting patiently, we leaned against the front fender and had a nice long smooching session. It left me longing for more physically but feeling a little better emotionally.

He leaned his forehead against mine. "Stay out of trouble, okay?" he whispered.

"Of course," I said with as much fake bluster as I could drum up, which wasn't much.

He shook his head slowly, then stooped down to give Buddy a goodbye pet. "Keep an eye on her, boy."

Buddy tilted his head and looked up at me. Will's eyes met mine and we both grinned.

I strapped Buddy into his harness in the backseat, then Will opened my driver's door and handed me into the car. "I'll call you tomorrow."

I was back at the Blacks' house, standing on their lanai while the dogs did their business in the backyard, when I remembered the unanswered call.

Probably a telemarketer. I pulled out my phone to clear it from recent calls and saw that the caller had left a message. Maybe it was Mattie's lawyer. My heart went into overdrive.

I called up voicemail and held the phone to my ear. Buddy and Felix were both running from tufts of grass to bushes to the bases of trees, noses down, searching out the perfect spot.

A deep, menacing voice rumbled in my ear. "You need to back off, lady. Before you get hurt."

CHAPTER TEN

My hand shook as I lowered the phone from my ear. I staggered two steps and dropped onto a wooden chaise lounge.

Suddenly I had the front half of an eighty-pound dog in my lap. Felix leaned his shoulder gently against my chest, turning his head to give me a soulful look.

I let out a shaky laugh. I'd been planning on doing a refresher training session or two with him, but had wondered how I would drum up the adrenaline to signal him. He was trained to respond to the scent of human anxiety.

The deep pressure was helping. My anxiety was going down. I didn't really understand how it worked. I wasn't sure the scientists even understood it, but deep pressure seemed to soothe the nervous system. It had first been used with autistic kids, I think, but now was used, in a variety of forms, for PTSD and other anxiety disorders.

Thinking about deep pressure therapy was also helping to distract my brain.

Buddy trotted over, stopping a few feet away. He cocked his head in his what's-up expression. He knew better than to interrupt a training session, but I guess he was trying to figure out if that's what this was.

I held out a hand in his direction. He took two steps and licked my fingers.

I sucked in a deep breath and let it out slowly, feeling my heart rate slowing to normal.

"I'm okay now, boy." I patted Felix on the head. "Down."

He slid off of me and settled beside the chaise, waiting for more instructions.

I stood and gestured for the dogs to follow me. Once inside I double-checked all the doors and the window locks.

I looked down at my two behemoth canine companions, panting with tongues hanging out. "Let's hope your mere presence is enough to discourage Mr. Gruff Voice." Since service dogs are specifically trained to ignore their territorial and protective instincts, they might or might not bark if someone broke into the house. And although they would put themselves between me and an approaching person, they would do nothing to discourage said person from attacking me.

Once such an attack was underway, I liked to think that Buddy would come to my defense, but I suspected he wouldn't. He was too well trained.

After all, I'd trained him.

Ironically, the anonymous threat had the exact opposite effect from the one the caller desired. It proved to me that Jake and Janey were innocent. I went to bed determined to find out who this guy was and how he was connected to the pawn shop robberies and Elsie Belenky's death.

But I did set the alarm and leave every light in the house blazing.

By morning, I'd convinced myself that there was no point in worrying about the Buddy situation for now. Mattie would do her darnedest to find a solution that didn't involve me losing him. And if she couldn't, well that would be time to worry.

So I opted to focus on Jake and Janey's predicament.

Sergeant Phelps had told me not to come around, but I now had his cell number, since he'd called me. As soon as I'd finished my breakfast cereal the next morning, I called him.

"Hello." He didn't sound happy.

"Look, I know you can't directly help me, but I'm gonna say

some things and you just say yes or no."

A brief beat of silence. A phone rang in the background. "Okay," Phelps finally said.

"You don't think Jake and Janey did all this, do you?"

"No."

"But you don't know who did?"

"Correct."

"You think it's a couple of bikers from the Dark Demons gang maybe?"

"Maybe."

Okay, this cryptic stuff wasn't working as well as I'd thought it would. My mind groped for more questions to ask. "Your eye-witnesses, they only saw the bikes, not the robbers' faces?"

"Correct."

"One of them recognized Jake's bike?"

"No."

"They just described the bikes, so who identified them as Jake and Janey's?"

Silence stretched out, broken by another phone ringing and the muffled kathunk-kathunk of a copy machine.

Wait, Phelps had said that he rode with Jake. "You identified them, didn't you?"

The sound of air being sucked in. "Afraid so."

Feeling desperate, I blurted out, "Look, I've put out some feelers, but I'm no detective. I need some guidance here. What else should I be doing?"

The sound of a door closing. The background noises disappeared. "That's not a yes-or-no question."

This time, I let the silence spin out.

He cleared his throat. "Well, normally during the course of an investigation, we would canvas the neighbors."

"Whose neighbors? Jake's?"

"No. We already did that."

"And no one saw anybody around Jake's garage the other day?"

"Correct." Apparently even behind a closed door, he wasn't willing to say much.

I stared across the Blacks' kitchen, trying to decipher what Phelps was trying to tell me. "The neighbors at the pawn shop?"

He blew out air. "Yes."

"Thank you, Sergeant."

"You're welcome, ma'am. Call any time."

A warm tide washed through me—relief, gratitude. I wasn't in this alone after all. "Thank you very, very much."

"Be careful." The sergeant disconnected.

People telling me to be careful was getting old. I knew I had to be careful, especially with Mr. Gruff Voice out there.

Feeling vaguely guilty, I put Buddy's service vest on him so I could take him along. It really wasn't kosher, since I wasn't disabled and I wasn't training a dog, but I couldn't bring myself to leave him home.

I drove us to the strip mall where the pawn shop was located.

I need not have worried about Buddy's reception. The merchants of the shopping center were used to Jake's service dog.

The pawn shop was closed, not surprising. On one side of it was a clothing boutique, with mannequins in the windows wearing styles I'd worn in high school. I began with the laundromat on the other side.

The owner, Phillip Sanford, was a pale, white guy in a light green knit shirt and khaki shorts. He had a receding hairline and a pronounced over bite. He looked like an aging Bugs Bunny.

He didn't bat an eye when I walked in with Buddy. I introduced myself and explained that I was a friend of the Blacks.

"Sure, I know them. They came in a few times a couple of months ago, when their washer went up on them. And Janey was in a week or so ago." He puffed his chest out some. "She was tryin' to get a grease stain outta her husband's dog's vest, like the one your dog's wearin'. She asked for my advice."

I smiled at him and he beamed back. He seemed a simple soul.

His expression sobered when I asked about the Belenkys next door. He gave a sad shake of his head. "I stop over a couple of times a day and check on them. They're really too old to be tryin' to run that place by themselves."

"Mr. Belenky said something about diamonds, that the thieves got them."

His eyebrows went up. "I knew he had some diamonds, but I didn't hear nothin' about them bein' taken. Izzy shouldn't be handlin' stuff like that. Not in this neighborhood."

"What do you mean 'not in this neighborhood?'"

Mr. Sanford walked to the door of the laundromat. Buddy and I followed. I looked where he was pointing. A one-story building across A1A from the shopping center had a long row of motorcycles lined up in front of it.

"It was only a matter of time," Sanford said, "'til one of them bikers decided the Belenkys was an easy target."

"Did you see anything the day of the first robbery?"

"Yeah, an' I tole the police all about it." He puffed out his chest again. "I saw this big guy with a ski mask coverin' his face run out of Izzy's store. He was wearin' a biker's helmet, and a black leather jacket. Then a woman came runnin' after him. She had somethin' over her face too an' a helmet. An' a black jacket. They jumped on their bikes and roared off."

"The guy had what colored hair?"

Sanford paused, stared up at the ceiling for a moment. "Dark." *Hmm...*

"And the woman?"

"She was a blonde," he said with more confidence.

"How could you see her hair?"

Sanford gave me a startled look. "It was stickin' out the bottom of her helmet, in the back."

"Was the guy's hair sticking out in the back?"

Sanford seemed confused for a moment. "Yeah, musta been."

"The woman, was she heavyset, skinny or somewhere in between?"

"Um, maybe between heavyset and somewhere in between."

If he was describing Janey, he was being gracious. She'd be considered heavyset by most people's standards. But I suspected Mr. Sanford was making half of this up as he went along. If the male robber had been Jake, his buzz cut certainly wouldn't be sticking out the bottom of his helmet.

Sanford's motives probably weren't malevolent though. Most likely he only wanted to prolong his moment of glory.

"What did their bikes look like?" I asked.

"His was black, big, with funny-lookin' fenders. Hers was a three-wheeled job, red, real broad across the rear end."

"His fenders were funny-looking how?"

"They had metal comin' partway down the wheel, like a little skirt."

My muscles tensed. That sure described the fenders on Jake's Indian motorcycle.

"Did you see their license plates?"

"Hers was too far away and his had something on it. Mud maybe."

"Did you see them ride out of the parking lot?"

"Yeah, the big guy, he spun out on a patch of sand and dumped his bike. He got up and pulled it up, jumped on and took off."

"When he got up, how did he do that?"

The man looked confused again.

"Did he get up slowly and awkwardly or quick and smooth?"

"Oh, quick and smooth. He was on his feet, yanked that bike up and was outta here in a few seconds."

I thanked Mr. Sanford.

He nodded and reached out as if to pet Buddy.

I quickly held up a hand.

He jerked his own hand back. "Sorry, I forgot yer not supposed to pet service dogs."

I smiled and thanked him again.

At the boutique on the other side of the pawn shop, the two teenaged clerks also wanted to pet Buddy. I explained about not distracting service dogs while they were on duty. One girl seemed to understand but the other pouted. Both were clueless about the events next door.

The thin, young woman in the natural foods store one door further down was probably one of the sheriff's department's corroborating witnesses. She smiled at Buddy, standing quietly beside my left knee. "Yes, I saw those two run out of the Belenkys' shop. The guy was big, at least two-forty. The woman was running funny, like fat women do sometimes, kinda waddling. She had her arms wrapped around herself."

"Could you see their faces?"

"No they had something covering them. They were covered from head to toe, all in dark clothing. Boots, blue jeans, leather jackets, helmets."

"Did you see their motorcycles?" I asked.

She shook her head. "No, I had a customer at the time so I couldn't leave the shop. It's not the first time the Belenkys have been robbed."

I didn't think familiarity of the criminal event quite justified not bothering to try to get a glimpse of a license plate. But then again, she would've had to run past three shops to see the parking lot.

"How about a couple of days ago, when they were robbed again?"

The woman's face pulled down into a sad frown. "You mean when Elsie was killed?"

I nodded, my stomach twisting again at the memory.

The woman shook her head slowly. "Things were a little busy here, and I didn't know anything was happening until the ambulance and the sheriff's deputies arrived."

I worked my way down several shops in each direction. Three other people had witnessed at least one of the robbers' getaways. They all described the same thing—a big man and a heavyset woman, both dressed in dark clothing and motorcycle helmets, running away from the pawn shop. Only one woman had seen the motorcycles, and she gave the same description of a black bike with odd-looking fenders and a red trike.

I asked if the woman was holding herself in a funny way. One witness shook his head, said he couldn't remember. Two of them wrapped their arms around their stomachs.

As Buddy and I walked back to my car, I observed several heavyset women.

None of them were holding their bellies, not even the one who was glancing at her watch and walking fast.

Once in the car, I called Jojo, wondering if I was being an idiot. He answered and I identified myself, then asked, "You know that bar on A1A, across from the pawn shop?"

"Yeah." His voice sounded wary.

"Can you take me there?"

A long pause. "I can, but I ain't sure that's a real good idea."

"Is it just a Demons' hangout, or are other bikers likely to be there too?"

"Mostly Demons, but it's early yet. At lunchtime, there'll be some others too."

Other wannabes like Jojo, most likely. Which wasn't all that reassuring.

"So, are these guys likely to attack me or something?" I asked.

"Probably not, if you're with me, but…" He trailed off.

"But what?"

"Ya gotta pretend that yer my ole lady."

Twenty minutes later, I'd dropped Buddy back at the Blacks' and hastily changed into jeans and a baggy tee-shirt I'd brought to sleep in. I didn't want to look too attractive.

I raced back to the shopping center to meet Jojo.

He straddled his Harley and held it steady as I awkwardly climbed on the back. I had some trouble getting my leg up over the saddlebags.

Now what? People I'd seen riding on the backs of motorcycles usually had their arms around the driver's waist. I stared at the

THE CALL OF THE WOOF

back of Jojo's leather vest. It looked like it hadn't been cleaned in this century.

I really didn't want to touch it, much less smush myself against it, and I wasn't at all sure my arms would reach around his waist. And where would I put my hands—against his bare belly?

I squelched a shudder as Jojo eased the bike across the crowded parking lot, dodging a few pedestrians.

At the exit, he suddenly surged forward, leaning the bike into the left turn.

Letting out a yelp, I grabbed for the sides of my seat, fingernails digging into the leather. Didn't these things have seatbelts?

Heart in my throat, I prayed harder than I had in years, while Jojo casually wove in and out of traffic for half a block and then turned into the bar's parking lot.

Coming to a stop, he said over his shoulder, "Climb off."

My heart still racing, I tried to oblige, but my foot caught on the seat.

He heaved a sigh, reached back a meaty hand and dislodged my sneaker.

I stumbled backward, almost falling on my keister.

Jojo dismounted, shook his shaggy head at me, and led the way into the building.

Smoky and dingy would have been accolades for this place. The smell of stale beer was strong. I swallowed hard, stifling my gag response, and followed Jojo to the bar.

Several tough-looking bikers, wearing jeans, tattoos, and leather or denim vests—some over short-sleeved shirts, some not—were scattered along the stools.

We found two stools together and planted ourselves on them. Jojo ordered two beers and burgers. I wasn't about to argue with either. I'd have preferred an iced tea but I suspected such a request would draw undue attention.

"Which ones are the Demons?" I whispered.

Jojo tilted his head slightly toward the other end of the bar. I noted the emblem on the backs of their vests—on a circle of red, a caricature of a black demon with gleaming red eyes and pointed ears, or maybe they were supposed to be horns. He was clutching silver motorcycle handlebars. The words *Dark Demons* adorned a red half-circle patch above him, with *Florida* on a similar patch curving upward below him.

"Don't stare," Jojo hissed under his breath.

"Sorry," I whispered. "What's that on their backs?"

"Their colors," Jojo said, in a tone that clearly conveyed that was a stupid question.

The barkeep brought our beers. Jojo took a hefty swig. I pretended to drink from mine.

I like to think I'm not a prude, despite my upbringing, but some of the words flying around the room made my ears burn. I discreetly watched the men—and they were mostly men—but at least half of them matched the description I'd gotten from the witnesses at the shopping center, big and wearing black leather.

I also listened, trying to pick Mr. Gruff Voice out of the crowd. There were a lot of deep voices but none that sounded quite like his.

Our burgers arrived. Mine was surprisingly good. We ate them slowly, while eavesdropping on nearby conversations.

One of the bikers at the other end of the bar broke loose from the group and sauntered our way. His main feature was a massive dark mustache. "Hey Jojo, what's happenin'?"

"Nothin' much, Ray. What's up with you?"

Ray just nodded and leered at me. "Who's this?"

"My ole lady, Markie."

I was used to people mangling my name, so I wasn't sure if he was intentionally disguising it or not. Either way, my heart rate had kicked up several notches.

Ray tipped an imaginary hat. "How do, Markie."

"Hi," I said.

"How ya been, Ray?" Jojo asked, no doubt trying to draw his attention away from me.

"Not bad, not bad." The man leered at me again.

I took a bite of my burger, staring straight ahead at the smeared mirror behind the bar. Chewing was difficult with a dry mouth, swallowing even harder.

"You hear about the latest robbery over at Izzy's place?" Jojo said.

Greasy leather vest and all, I wanted to hug him in that moment.

A restless stirring rippled down the bar. Ray frowned, his mustache drooping.

"Yeah, man," a biker a couple of stools over said. "It sucks that his ole lady was killed."

Murmurs up and down the bar, the gist of which was that Izzy was okay.

"Whoever did that was a total s.o.b.," Jojo declared in a loud voice.

More murmurs of ascent, but no new information.

"I wanna know if anybody's got any idea who did that?" Jojo said, his pitch rising even more. He must have realized he sounded a bit hysterical, because he added in a quieter voice, "Izzy's a good guy, always gives me a fair deal when I need ta pawn stuff."

More murmurs up and down the bar.

"Come on." Jojo took my elbow and pulled me toward the door.

I didn't resist.

CHAPTER ELEVEN

But once outside, I regretted my passivity. "I should have tried to question some of them."

Jojo was tugging me along by my arm. He stopped halfway across the parking lot and turned to me.

"No, ya shouldn't 've," he said in a low voice. "They ain't exactly big on women's lib in there. But I planted us some seeds. If anybody's gonna tell me anythin', it'll be more likely in private anyway."

Movement caught my eye. I looked toward the bar. One of the bikers was striding in our direction—jeans, light denim shirt, black leather vest, weathered skin, and a red doo-rag tied around his dark hair.

"Hey, Loo," Jojo said.

"Hey," the biker replied, smacking Jojo on the shoulder. "Good seein' ya, man."

Jojo grinned, obviously pleased to have garnered this man's attention. They exchanged pleasantries for a few minutes, riddled with bike lingo that I only half understood.

Then the guy, Lou, shook his head. "That is a cryin' shame 'bout Elsie."

Jojo's mouth pulled down.

"Ain't right," Lou said, "somebody bashin' an ole lady on the head like that. Me an' the boys'll do some sniffin' around. We'll give you a shout if we find out anythin'."

Jojo's smile came back. "'Preciate that."

The man nodded slightly in my direction, then turned on his heel and went back toward the bar, which surprised me some. I'd assumed he was heading for his bike to leave and stopped to chat, but he'd made a special trip outside just to talk to Jojo.

Proving Jojo's point about seeds and privacy.

"So, what's this Louis's last name?" I asked once the guy was out of earshot.

Jojo chuckled. "Not Louis. Loo as in lieutenant. He's second in command in the Demons."

"Oh." I processed that for a second. "These guys don't seem all that scary."

"That's cuz yer with me and yer not law enforcement or a rival gang member. Most of 'em come across as nice guys, and they are, in a way. But don't go gettin' any ideas. You come around here by yerself, especially after dark…" He trailed off.

I thanked Jojo but begged off from the bike ride back across A1A. It was far safer for me to walk, but I didn't tell him that.

He got on his bike, gave me a small salute, and took off.

I walked to the nearest corner. But before I tackled crossing the busy street, I took out my phone and listened again to Mr. Gruff Voice's message. I played it several times, shuddering a little less with each time.

There's something to be said for exposure therapy.

Best I could remember from the voices in the bar, none of them were a match.

But I did realize something I hadn't when I'd first listened to the message last night. It sounded like the guy was intentionally deepening his voice, trying to disguise it.

I was halfway home before it occurred to me to wonder how Loo knew the cause of Elsie's death. I didn't remember it being mentioned in the news reports. But then again, Larry knew since he'd actually been there, and the biker world probably had a pretty good grapevine.

That afternoon, I visited Janey, as I'd promised Jake I would.

But also because it had occurred to me that I should be checking out any enemies Jake had.

She was pale but otherwise seemed to be holding her own. I picked up the phone on my side of the glass barrier and told her that Jake was okay and Felix missed them both.

"Janey, is there anyone you can think of who would want to frame you and Jake for this?"

She gave a slight shake of her head. "No, we get along fine with everybody."

That didn't surprise me. They were both easy-going people, except when Jake's TBI set his temper off.

"Is there anybody that Jake's had a conflict with, since he's been home? Because of the TBI maybe?"

"Nothing serious. He tries not to let it come out at people. Mostly he gets frustrated with inanimate objects or he just rages in general. At home, though. Never out in public. He threw a boot at the TV one time because he didn't like something on the news." She smiled a little. "Fortunately, he missed."

"Does he really have that much control over the anger?"

Her cheeks turned pink. "Well, now he does. The other day was the worst I've seen him in some time. When he first came home, he wouldn't leave the house for fear he'd go off on somebody. He had a few minor tiffs with service people who came to fix things at the house. But I took them aside and explained about the TBI."

None of that felt grudge-worthy, especially not enough to frame someone for robbery and murder. "How about old enemies?" I asked.

Janey gave another slight head shake, but there was a minute shift in her eyes—so quick I thought maybe I'd imagined it.

"Are you sure?"

"Yeah. We get along fine with everybody now."

Which really wasn't quite answering the question, since I'd asked about old enemies.

But before I could push her, she said, "Have you heard from

our daughter?"

Confused by the change of subject, I shook my head. "No."

"Good." Janey's eyes pooled with tears. She gripped the phone receiver tighter. "If she calls, tell her everything is okay."

"But it's not," I blurted out.

"She's doing a study-abroad this semester, in Italy. No point in disrupting that."

Crapola. I prayed Andrea didn't call, because then I'd have to make a tough choice. Personally I'd want to know if my parents were in jail for murder.

I stared into Janey Black's still shiny eyes. "Promise me," she said.

"She's not a child." I tried to keep my tone gentle.

"She's *my* child," Janey said fiercely. "Promise me you won't tell her."

I had trouble fathoming that fierceness in normally mild-mannered Janey. Her life was falling apart around her, but all she could think about was keeping her daughter's studies from being disrupted.

Would I be that protective and selfless?

I sighed. "I won't contact her, but if she calls the house, I won't lie to her."

Janey pressed her lips together in a tight line. "Thanks for coming, Marcia."

She started to hang up the phone, but Southern manners must have overridden her anger. She brought the receiver back to her face. "And thanks for watching Felix and the house."

"You're welcome. Take care of yourself."

As I was leaving the jail, a young woman and I converged on the door at the same time. She held a baby on one hip and a three or four-year-old girl by the hand.

I grabbed the door handle and held it open, then followed them out.

The little girl stopped and turned back toward me. She wore a sky blue sundress and little white sandals. "Were you visiting my daddy too?"

I stooped down. "No, I was visiting a friend of mine."

Her dark eyes were wide and solemn. "Daddy can't come home tomorrow, and it's my birthday."

My eyes stung even as I wondered what foolhardy thing her father had done to get himself locked up. I wanted to crush this little girl against my chest and tell her everything would be okay, but of course I didn't.

Her mom tugged gently on her hand, gave me a small smile, and the family—minus husband and father—walked away.

"Happy birthday," I called after them.

The little girl turned her head and smiled at me. Her mom leaned over a little and spoke to her. "Thank you," the child called out and waved.

My throat tight, I waved back.

I was headed back to the Blacks' house to check on the dogs—even with the signs on the doors, I was feeling a bit paranoid—when my mother called.

"You finally get a landline and then you don't answer it," her voice complained from my Bluetooth speaker.

"Sorry, Mom. Remember that work I told you I needed to have done on the house? They're doing it this week. I'm staying, um, at a friend's place, over on the coast."

"What *um, friend*? Marcia, you didn't break up with that nice sheriff, did you?"

Dang, was there some code or something that required mothers to pick up on every little nuance?

"No. I'm dog and house-sitting for a former client."

We exchanged pleasantries and I dutifully asked about my brother and his family. I was told they were all fine.

"Say Mom, it would make you really happy, wouldn't it, if I had kids?"

The briefest of pauses. "Yes, but not if having them made you unhappy. Kids are a huge responsibility."

"And you don't think I can handle it."

"Of course, you can handle it."

"But you always said I was irresponsible."

A low chuckle. "Marcia, that was when you were a child yourself. All kids are irresponsible. It's a parent's job to teach them responsibility, plus a whole lot of other things."

I let out a small sigh. "Well, *I'm* not sure I could handle it."

"None of us are, and thank God we don't completely realize what we're getting into ahead of time. But most folks rise to the occasion."

You're not really helping, Mom.

"But if you don't, rise to the occasion that is, there's no going back."

Another brief pause. "No, there isn't." Her voice was softer but more serious. "You'd make a great mother, Marcia. But you've got to do it because you want to, not to please me or Will or anybody else."

Was it that I didn't *want* children, or that I was afraid? I wasn't sure I was ready to ask that question out loud.

Mom and chatted a few more minutes and then said our good-byes, as I was turning onto Jake's street.

I pulled up in front of the house and adrenaline shot through me. A strange motorcycle was parked in the middle of the Blacks' driveway.

Mr. Gruff Voice?

My survival instinct said to stay put and call the police, but fear that the owner of that bike might have done something to the dogs propelled me out of my car. Blood pounding in my ears, I crept cautiously up the sidewalk.

I came to an abrupt stop when I realized a man was standing, his back to me, in the shadows on the front porch. He wore a black leather jacket and dark blue helmet. A gloved finger reached out and punched the doorbell button.

I backed slowly away.

Then he turned toward me.

I took off running back to my car.

"Wait, Marcia. It's me."

I slowed and pivoted back around.

Larry Merrick had stepped off the porch and into the sunlight. He stood there grinning, his hair slick with sweat from the helmet that was now balanced against his hip.

He took two steps toward me. "I know it's early but I wanted to catch you before you ate supper. You wanna take a ride with me?"

"Uh, I told you, I'm involved."

"It's not a date, although food will be involved. I thought it might be helpful if you met some of the guys, and gals, in the clubs around town. Best way to do that is to go to dinner at one of their favorite haunts."

He lifted the helmet in the air. "I've got an extra one of these. You okay with riding on the back of the bike? It's not far."

I hadn't heard from Will all day. I wasn't sure what that meant. Probably nothing other than he was having a busy day. But it was now four o'clock, so obviously he and I weren't getting together tonight for dinner.

"Yeah, I guess. Lemme check on the dogs."

While the brief stint on Jojo's bike had been hair-raising, riding on the back of Larry's motorcycle turned out to be exhilarating.

He'd insisted I change from my capris and sandals into jeans and sneakers. "If we go down," he held his hand up in a stop gesture, as if I'd voiced a protest, "which is unlikely, but if we do, you don't want bare skin meeting the road surface. A jacket would be good too."

My insides had relaxed some at that point. His precautions reassured me that he was a more responsible biker than Jojo, and I wouldn't have the same objections to holding onto him.

I didn't have a jacket with me, so I'd borrowed one of Janey's from their coat closet. Yes, most Florida houses have such closets near the front door, although they're usually tiny.

The too-big leather jacket flapped in the wind as we sped down A1A, and I found myself laughing.

I jerked a little when Larry's voice said in my ear. "Fun, isn't it?"

"You can hear me?"

"Helmets are wired for sound."

"Awesome," I said and hung onto his waist as he rounded a curve.

The ride was indeed only a few minutes long. My disappointment surprised me. I could get hooked on that feeling of freedom and excitement.

I was also surprised by our destination. Larry helped me off the bike and we both removed our helmets.

"Cracker Barrel?" I asked.

"Yup." He grinned at me. "It's a bikers' favorite."

For the next couple of hours, Larry held court—there was no better term for it—at a center table in the Cracker Barrel, as we worked our way through two orders of ribs and sides.

Most of the men came over of their own accord. Some he waved over. A few were in their forties. A few were thin. But most were fifty-plus and well-padded, with mostly plump, middle-aged wives in tow.

They greeted Larry—Bach they called him—with handshakes and back slaps and then shot the breeze until their wives got antsy. Somewhere in there as subtly as he could, Larry would ask if they'd seen or heard of any new bikers in town. Or had they heard of anything going on with the Dark Demons?

I didn't have much to do except smile and nod when Larry introduced me as a friend of Jake and Janey. I was starting to get antsy myself, when I saw a familiar face come through the door. Larry was busy chatting up yet another biker.

I excused myself, implying I was going to the ladies' room. Instead, I crossed the room to a booth along the side wall, where the waitress had just handed a menu to the sole occupant.

The man looked up as I approached. "Whadaya want?"

Snarky me jumped out and took over. "And good evening to you, Detective Wright. It's such a fine evening, don't you think?"

He rolled his eyes. "Ya got a reason for hovering over my table when I'm off duty?" I could definitely detect the New Jersey in his voice.

I wrestled Ms. Snarky behind me. "May I sit down?"

"No."

I did anyway, on the bench across from him. "Look, I'm sorry we got off on the wrong foot." I wasn't really sorry, since I doubted I was responsible for his foul mood. But you get more bees with honey, and all that jazz. "I just wanted to talk to you about the Blacks' case."

The waitress approached, throwing confused glances in my direction. "Do you need more time, Detective?" Her use of his title implied he came here often.

"Nah." He slammed the menu shut. "Pulled pork with baked potato and cole slaw. And coffee."

She wrote on her pad. "And you, ma'am?"

"She ain't staying," Wright growled.

The waitress hurried off.

"So talk."

I took a deep breath. I hadn't really thought about what to say. "I think Jake's being framed," I blurted out.

"They're sure doing a swell job."

"Not really. All you have is circumstantial evidence."

He smiled. Well, actually it looked more like a sneer. "No, we've got forensic evidence placing him there." He rubbed his fingers together.

"The sand?"

He nodded.

"But those aren't Jake's saddlebags."

"Says Jake."

On a hunch, I said, "Was there anything in them?"

He looked a little startled. "No."

"Don't you think that odd, that a biker would have nothing in his bags? Not even a wrench or screwdriver to work on his bike if he broke down?"

His expression shifted to a neutral mask, his cop face. Which meant I'd probably scored a point.

"Ms. Banks, I'm on my own time here. May I enjoy my dinner in peace?"

As if on cue, the waitress arrived with his coffee.

I waited until she had left, then said, "Thank you for your time, Detective." I pushed to a stand.

"You're welcome," he said.

I'd just about decided that maybe he was human after all, when his mouth curved into a sneer again. "See you around, Ms. Banks."

Not if I see you first.

I made myself walk calmly across the restaurant. Larry was chatting with a man and his wife so I kept moving. Now I really did need the ladies' room.

I followed the restroom sign to a hallway beside the kitchen, walked past the men's room on my left, and pushed open the door with the skirted stick figure on it. As I did my thing and then washed my hands, I thought about what I had that might clear the Blacks.

They were all negatives. Jake couldn't ride a two-wheeled bike. Fat ladies didn't hold their bellies when they ran. Bikers didn't ride around with empty saddlebags.

Frustrated, I stepped out of the ladies' room and walked along the hall toward the restaurant's dining room, my mind still mulling over the evidence.

An arm, clad in black leather, wrapped around my neck. "Let it go," a deep whisper in my ear, "if ya know what's good fer ya."

Then the arm was gone.

CHAPTER TWELVE

I whirled around. The men's room door flapped shut.

Between cowardice and thirty-some years of training that said girls and women did *not* go into a men's room, it took a few seconds of working up my nerve to push open that door.

Unfortunately, as I was tentatively pushing it, a man yanked it open from inside. I almost fell against him.

He jumped back half a step. "What are you doin', lady?"

My nerve fled, followed swiftly by the rest of me. "Sorry," I mumbled and scurried away. Shaken, I went back to our table, throwing glances over my shoulder at the entrance to the hallway under the restroom sign.

"There you are." Larry smiled brightly at me.

I sat down with a thud, then jumped when a waitress appeared out of nowhere.

"You want more coffee?" She held up a half-full pot.

Larry nodded.

I shook my head. Obviously, I was wired enough. Although who could blame me for being jumpy? It's not every day you're accosted coming from the ladies' room in a Cracker Barrel.

"That's probably the last of them," Larry was saying while stirring cream into his coffee. "Bikers are an early-to-bed lot. In Florida, you have to ride at the crack of dawn to beat the heat."

I reached for my water glass with a shaky hand. I took a sip, still watching the entrance to that hallway. Two women had come out, and one man went in.

I opened my mouth to tell Larry what had happened and ask him to go check out the men's room. Then I clamped it shut, realizing the futility of it. Leather jackets were common amongst bikers. Larry had crammed his into a case on the side of his bike when we'd arrived. And I had Janey's draped over the back of my chair.

I touched its sleeve and shuddered, my eyes still glued to the spot under that restroom sign.

Then it dawned on me that my assailant didn't have to come out this way. He could've gone out through the kitchen.

If only I'd had my wits about me… I should've waited around the corner at the end of the hall and discovered which way he went, maybe even gotten a look at his face.

Too late now. No doubt, he was long gone.

Again, I considered telling Larry, but something made me hold back. He might go all protective on me like Will and not be willing to help me anymore.

My mind, searching for distraction, landed on the Buddy issue. All things are relative. In the disasters-you're-trying-not-to-think-about category, losing your life trumps losing your dog.

"Hey, do you know a tax lawyer?" I asked.

Larry chuckled. "Yeah, me."

"Seriously? I thought because you represented Izzy Belenky that you were a criminal lawyer."

"Nah, I went with him as a friend. A favor. Didn't want the old guy to get confused and maybe say something the police would misinterpret."

"Honest, you're a tax lawyer?"

He nodded.

Maybe there was a God after all, because this sure felt like a sign to me.

"Wait a minute. I saw your ad on the phone book, with you rolling up your sleeves."

"I've started doing personal injury cases too. That's where the money is. So what's your tax problem?"

I told him as succinctly as possible, while keeping an eye on that hallway, just in case.

Surprise, surprise. No one came out wearing a leather jacket.

The motorcycle ride back to the house wasn't nearly as much fun. I kept reliving those moments in the restroom hallway.

Once home, I checked my phone for missed calls. Will had called and it had gone to voicemail.

Crapola.

It had never rung. Or maybe it did while we were on the bike and I hadn't heard it.

I listened to his message. "Hey, Marcia. Sorry, it's been one of those days. Give me a call when you get this."

I called him back. We made small talk for a few minutes while I kept shoving aside thoughts of Cracker Barrel hallways.

"Heard anything from Mattie about Buddy?" Will asked.

"No, but I found a tax lawyer who thinks he can help."

"That's great."

"He's that guy I told you about, Larry Merrick. The biker the sergeant sent me to."

"A biker who's a lawyer," Will said. "That's unusual."

"Actually, not as much so as you might think. I'm learning that most motorcycle enthusiasts are average citizens—plumbers, electricians, even professionals like lawyers."

"I hear you. I've known a few cops who were bikers."

"Sergeant Phelps is one. That's how he knows Jake and Larry."

"Have you talked to him again?"

I hesitated. The question was innocent enough. After all, I'd brought up Phelps's name. "Yeah, he pointed me toward the neighbors in the shopping center."

A far-too-long pregnant pause. "And you did what?"

I let a beat go by, trying to figure out how to get out of answering that. "Talked to them."

"What are you doing, Marcia? You're gonna get yourself hurt. Let Jake's attorney handle things."

"Why are you so sure I'll get hurt? Does that mean you think Jake is innocent?" A vice clamped around my heart. I hadn't told him about Mr. Gruff Voice's call, much less tonight's encounter with a leather jacket sleeve.

What would he think if he found out about those threats now?

A beat of silence on his end, then he said, "I dug up something else. There's been a whole string of robberies like the ones in Buckland Beach, over the last couple of years, up and down the coast. All bikers with their faces hidden. Mostly in pairs, sometimes a man and a woman, sometimes two men. I talked to the detective working the case in Flagler Beach. They've had three there, and in all three instances, the stores had just gotten in a shipment of something valuable."

He paused. My brain was churning, as was my stomach.

"This guy, the Flagler detective, he thinks there's someone pretty bright behind it all. Someone who has ways to find out about these shipments. Someone with good organizational and planning skills, say a local businessman ..." He trailed off.

I knew what he wasn't saying. *The owner of a big construction company maybe.*

But I really couldn't see Jake in that role. He didn't care all that much about money. The fact that his construction company grew so big was one part due to his compulsive perfectionism—he made sure his buildings were built right—and one part due to the rapid growth in the State of Florida. And now he had enough money that he certainly didn't need to run some theft ring in order to make more.

It registered that Will had fallen silent again. A horn sounded in the background.

"Are you driving?"

"Yeah."

"Where are you going?"

"Would you believe me if I said I was going to get drunk because my girlfriend is making me crazy with worry?"

I let out a small chuckle. "No."

"My night dispatcher called in sick. I have to go back to the station."

Most people don't realize that a police or sheriff's department can't have just anyone answer their emergency line—911 dispatchers receive specialized training and certification. And there's no filling in with an uncertified person if your dispatcher is sick. Will had been required to get the dispatcher training when he took office, so he could be the back-up person.

"I'm sorry," I said.

"Why? Because I have to work tonight or because you make me nuts?"

I chuckled again. "Both. Look, I'll be careful. I don't want to get hurt. Honest, I don't." I most definitely didn't want to get hurt, but I also didn't want Jake and Janey to go to prison for something they hadn't done, and if they got blamed for this whole string of robberies…

"Have you talked to your contractor lately?" Will asked.

"No, I was going to go over and check on the place tomorrow morning."

"Okay. Let me know how things are going."

His voice sounded funny. I held my breath, afraid he was about to bring up the living-together issue.

But he didn't. We made small talk for a few more minutes and then signed off.

I went in the kitchen to get a bottle of water from the fridge. The clock on the wall said six-fifty.

Really? This day might just break all records as the longest day of my life. It felt like a week since I'd set out to canvas the neighboring businesses around the pawn shop.

A loud ringing made me jump. I tracked the sound to a portable phone resting in its charger on the counter.

With a sense of dread, I checked caller ID. *Andrea Black.* I was tempted to let it go to voicemail, but I already felt like a coward for not tracking down Mr. Leather Jacket Sleeve.

Taking a deep breath, I punched the talk button. "Hello."

"Hey, Mom. Hope y'all weren't eating supper."

"Uh, this isn't your mother. I'm Marcia Banks, the woman who trained Felix."

"Oh? Yeah, okay." Her voice was tentative, but she recovered quickly. "Uh, we met last year, didn't we?"

"Yes." She'd been home for the weekend one of the times I'd come to work with Jake and Felix.

"How are you?" Andrea asked politely. Her folks had raised her right.

"I'm fine," I said, even though I was anything but. Every muscle in my body was tensed, waiting for the inevitable question.

"So where are Mom and Dad?"

"Um, I'm afraid they're in jail."

"What?" she yelled in my ear.

It took a few minutes to calm her down and fill her in, then another few to convince her to stay in Italy, for now at least. Her mother's desire that her studies not be disrupted didn't hold much sway.

"Look, a couple of investigators are working on the case." I didn't bother to mention that I was one of them, and a rank amateur. "I'm hopeful that they'll prove your parents' innocence in the next few days. Probably before you could even get here. Hey, isn't it the middle of the night over there?"

A feeble attempt to change the subject, but it worked.

"It is, but I'm a night owl. My classes are all in the afternoon."

"Let me ask you something, while I've got you. Do you know of any enemies your folks might have, past or present? Someone who'd want to frame them for this?" I hadn't been totally satisfied with her mother's answer to that question.

A brief pause. "I can't think of anyone who dislikes my parents. They get along with everybody."

"How about other construction companies?"

"Not that I know of, and Dad's not all that involved anymore. He has a general manager running things now."

So getting Jake in hot water wouldn't really change the

operation of the company. Even damaging his personal reputation probably wouldn't have all that much impact.

I blew out air. Andrea and I signed off after I promised to call her if there were any new developments.

I sat down at the kitchen table to mull things over. Did the Blacks truly have no enemies? Or was their daughter innocently unaware of any grudges from the past? It was possible Jake and Janey made convenient scapegoats only because they rode fairly distinctive-looking bikes.

That seemed more likely considering there'd been robberies in other towns with a similar M.O. This wasn't a localized crime spree by someone who had it in for Jake and Janey, but rather a well-organized operation that just happened to peg the Blacks as the best fall guys in Buckland Beach.

The clock on the wall now read seven-forty-five. I decided I didn't care if there was still a little light left in the sky. I was going to bed.

Early the next morning, I piled both dogs into my car and headed for home.

Normally I like to drive, find it soothing even, but today my nerves were on edge. I swear the butterflies in my stomach were taking salsa lessons.

And the long drive to Mayfair gave me way too much time to think. How would I pay for the extra repairs? Was I going to lose Buddy? Was Will going to get fed up with me if I wouldn't move in with him?

Were Mr. Gruff Voice and Mr. Leather Jacket Sleeve one and the same person? That seemed likely. Would he make good on his threats if I didn't leave the Blacks' case alone?

And what more could I do at this point anyway? We'd put out feelers with the bikers. Now came the waiting to see if anything interesting developed from that.

Hey, I hadn't talked to Izzy Belenky, except for that brief interchange at the sheriff's department. How would Mr. Leather

Jacket Sleeve know if I discreetly paid a visit to the pawn shop this afternoon?

As I drove into the town of Mayfair, I slowed to observe the progress on Edna's motel. The walls were finally going up. Until last week, all that had been accomplished was the cement slab base. But now a swarm of workmen were erecting sections of two-by-four studs and attaching backboards to them that would then be covered with a siding called Hardie board, which I'd never heard of until moving to Florida. Made of sand, cement and fiber, the siding was rot, insect and fire resistant. And considering Edna's and my recent misfortunes with the last two of those, she had decided it was worth the extra cost.

I pulled over and stopped. Staring at the bare-bones frame for a minute, I could discern the outline of the Victorian-style, two-story building it would become, with its wide veranda stretching across the front and down one side. Excitement bubbled in my chest, and in that moment, I vowed to do whatever I could to make the motel and the town a tourist attraction. Quaint rural Florida ought to sell as a weekend or vacation getaway.

I deflated as I remembered that I might be selling my house and moving to Collinsville.

I drove down Main Street to my house. There the hammering was almost as loud as at the motel site. I got out, let the dogs out of the backseat and grabbed Felix's service vest.

Sherie Wells, my next-door neighbor and the only African-American matriarch in the town, stepped out onto her front stoop as we headed up my sidewalk.

My house retained its original semi-shotgun design—living room in the front leading to kitchen to the left and two small bedrooms, with a bath in between, to the right. But the Wells's abode resembled a polyglot cargo train, with several additions strung out beside the cottage—in varying sizes and made from different building materials.

Sherie was the daughter-in-law of the first Mr. Wells of Mayfair, caretaker of the long since defunct Mayfair Alligator

Farm around which the town had originally developed in the 1960s.

Today, Sherie's still regal, sixty-something form was clad in a royal blue shirtwaist dress at least four decades out of style. White teeth flashed in her brown face. "Mornin', Marcia," she called out, loud enough to be heard over the racket.

"Morning," I yelled back.

There was a sudden lull in the construction noises.

"Phew, how long am I gonna be blessed with stereophonic hammering?" Sherie asked, but her smile was warm.

"Not too much longer on my side, I hope, 'cause every day they're banging, my bank account is shrinking."

"Is that Felix?" Sherie gestured toward the big brindle-coated dog but made no move to pet him. She knew better, unless she was sure the animal was off duty.

"Yeah, I'm dog-sitting temporarily."

"You want some sweet tea?"

"Can I take you up on that in about an hour? Lemme check in with my contractor and I'll have a better answer to your how-long question by then."

She nodded as the hammering on my roof resumed.

I went in through my front door and gestured for the dogs to go into the two large crates lined up against my living room wall.

The exterminator had assured me that the gas used in the fumigation would leave no residue, but I had to resist the urge to grab a sponge and wipe down everything in sight.

I closed the crate doors and went through the kitchen to the backyard. I wanted to make sure there were no nails or other sharp debris lying about before I let the dogs out there. As I'd suspected, the yard close to the house was littered with broken shingles, splintered pieces of wood, and no doubt many bent nails buried in the grass.

I glared up at the roof where Pete, my contractor, and his men were pounding away.

My anger was somewhat mollified when I saw how much

progress they'd made. Clean, new wood covered two-thirds of the back part of the roof. The sounds shifted from banging to the thump-thump of a nail gun, as they began to attach tar paper to the wood.

Pete noticed me standing in the middle of the yard and waved. Then he trotted down the gentle slope of the roof and clambered down a ladder.

He jogged up to me. "How ya doin', Marcia?"

"I'm okay, Pete, but my bank account is in cardiac arrest."

His chuckle had a nervous edge. "It won't be too awful, and now you know you've got a good solid roof that will last for years."

"Did you have to tear all the back shingles off?"

He gave me a funny look. "Uh, 'fraid so, to make sure we'd gotten all the damaged wood. By end of the day tomorrow, we'll have it all done and you can get back in here. You got someplace to stay, right?"

I nodded, wondering a little at his concern about that. Technically, I could move back in now, but I didn't relish the idea of the constant pounding over my head for the next two days. And I didn't want to abandon Jake and Janey anyway.

I couldn't stay at their place for too much longer though. I had to get started training a new dog soon, so that my mortally-wounded bank account had at least a shot at recovery.

That reminded me that I'd intended to do some refresher training with Felix while we were here. I debated about doing that with the distraction of the construction going on. But maybe that would be good, to see if Felix stayed focused despite all the noise and chaos.

I walked over and unlocked the gate in the six-foot fence. No way I was bringing the dog through that minefield of construction debris. Then I went back through the house and brought him around the side, in his specialized service dog vest.

In the back part of my yard, I put him through the basics, especially the cover position, which I knew the veterans sometimes neglected to reinforce. I walked him across the far end of the backyard, stopping at erratic intervals. Each time he took up his position, sitting facing behind me but where I could see his signal should someone approach.

Normally that signal would be a single distinct wag of the dog's tail or their ears perking up. But since his tail was barely more than a stub and his ears weren't much bigger, I'd devised a different signal for Felix. He was supposed to point his nose high in the air.

Which is just what he did when I stopped a few feet from the far end of the yard, my back to the house.

I pivoted around. Dexter Mayfair was striding toward me across the lawn.

Felix immediately inserted himself between me and Dexter, not in an aggressive way, but as he'd been taught to do, to maintain his master's personal space.

"Good boy," I crooned softly and gave him a treat from my pocket.

"Hey, Marcia," Dexter said. "Aunt Edna thought she saw ya out here. Can ya stop on over before ya go?"

"Sure."

He turned and jogged back across the yard, leaving me wondering what Edna wanted.

I brought my attention back to Felix. "You're such a good boy."

I headed back in the direction of the house. After a few paces, I faked a stagger. I'd seen Felix respond to Jake's instability a few days ago, even though he hadn't even been in his vest. But still I wanted to test him, and also reward him to reinforce the behavior.

Sure enough, the dog immediately braced himself to take my weight as I leaned heavily on the curved bar sticking up from the top of his vest—a vest specially made for dogs partnered with veterans suffering from traumatic brain injury.

A little further along, I faked another stagger. The dog spread his legs to brace himself. I leaned on the support bar again, then gave him another treat.

His deep pressure response to anxiety had already been tested twice in the last forty-eight hours, so I was very well pleased.

I knelt beside him and gave his ears a hearty scratch. "You are such a good boy."

He looked at me out of those soulful eyes, then licked my hand.

We headed back toward the house. Suddenly my ankle went out from under me.

I grabbed for the bar on Felix's vest and he braced himself. Thank heavens I hadn't removed the vest yet.

I examined the spot where I'd stepped. It was bare, sandy dirt and soft. My foot had made a deep indentation. Probably a mole had been burrowing there.

I made a mental note to get some top soil from the hardware store and fill in the hole.

CHAPTER THIRTEEN

As I took Felix back around to the front of the house, Edna appeared on Sherie Wells's stoop, as if she'd been waiting for me. Today's muumuu featured large blossoms that looked like camelias, although I'd never seen that particular flower in quite that shade of neon orange. I spared a moment to wonder how she had so readily replenished her supply of wacky muumuus.

She grinned at me. "There you are, Marcia."

"Be right over." I took Felix inside, put him in a crate and gave him fresh water and a dental chew treat. As I headed back for the door, he was happily slobbering over the latter.

Buddy rose from the bed in the other crate. I was about to tell him to stay when suddenly my throat closed. Who knew how much longer I'd have him with me? I opened the crate door and signaled for him to follow me.

We went out the front door and across the strip of lawn to Sherie's front porch.

Edna opened the door before I could knock.

"Hey, Buddy," she exclaimed as if it had been a month rather than a few days since she'd seen him last. She bent down and patted his head, then scratched his ears.

His expression was blissful, eyes closed, nose high in the air. My throat closed again.

We stepped into Sherie's crowded living room. Not only had each Wells generation built onto the house but they'd also added furniture. And getting rid of anything seemed to be a family taboo.

Sherie beamed at me from across the room. "I'll get the tea." She turned toward the kitchen.

What the heck? Sherie Wells rarely *beamed* at anyone.

Edna perched on the edge of a loveseat and gestured for me to sit on the adjacent sofa. She was beaming too, but that was much less out of character.

As Buddy settled at my feet, she said, "So, how's Will?"

That threw me a little. I'd expected the first question to be about how long Pete and his boys would be banging on my roof.

"He's fine."

Sherie returned with a tray. She set it down on her coffee table. "Unsweetened," she said, pointing to the glass pitcher.

"Thanks." I really appreciated that she'd remembered my distaste for sweet tea. It might be a Southern staple and technically I was now a Southerner, but I would never get used to iced tea that was as sweet as Kool-Aid.

Sherie poured and then we took turns doctoring our glasses with varying amounts of sugar from the crystal bowl on the tray.

Edna dumped three teaspoons into her tea. "So, you two got any plans, once your house is done?"

I cocked my head in her direction.

"You know," Sherie said, a tad hastily, "to travel or whatever?"

"No. I'm looking forward to getting back into some kind of routine. And I need to get started with a new dog. No training means no income." I might even attempt to start two dogs at once. That would be challenging, since I usually had one dog's training almost completed when I started another dog on the basics. But I had to reverse the flow of funds *into* my bank account pretty soon here.

Speaking of no income... "Hey, I saw that the motel construction is coming along."

Edna actually bounced up and down in her seat. "Yes, finally it's gettin' done."

I expected her to elaborate. Normally it didn't take much to get Edna talking. But she and Sherie each took sips from their tea as they stared at me, expectant expressions on their faces.

Okay, this was getting weird.

"Pete said he'd be done in a couple of days."

They both broke out big grins, which struck me as more enthusiasm than the news merited. But then again, I hadn't been living next door to the incessant hammering like they had.

"Well, I guess we'll see you back here then," Sherie said, her head bobbing in a nod.

"Yeah." I nodded back, wondering how my usually comfortable relationship with my neighbors had become so stilted.

I put my now empty glass back on the tray. "Well, I'd better get going." I also only had two days left to solve Elsie Belenky's murder.

Sherie rose and saw me and Buddy to the door. "Tell Will hi for us."

"Yeah," Edna called out from the loveseat. "Tell him we're lookin' forward to seein' him around more."

"To seeing both of you around again," Sherie quickly added.

"Sure. See you soon."

Once out on the stoop with the door closed, I looked down at Buddy. "Okay, that was strange."

He tilted his head to one side.

I was halfway back to Jake's, both dogs snoozing in the backseat, when my phone rang. What did I ever do before Bluetooth?

No name attached to the number, but again it was a local area code. I answered.

A gravelly voice said, "Hello?"

I almost drove off the road.

"That you, Mz. Markie?"

I accepted the mangling of my name this time because it told me who the caller was—not Mr. Gruff Voice after all. "Jojo?"

"Yes, ma'am. I think I might have somethin' for you. Loo called to tell me that one of the Demons is lookin' to sell his bike cuz he just bought a brand spankin' new one. Top of Harley's line too."

"Okay," I said, wondering how this was a lead.

"Well, this boy Rusty, he don't usually have two nickels to rub together, but suddenly he's buyin' a new bike."

"Oh. That *is* interesting." Something was niggling at me though.

"Yeah. I figured we could go over there and I'd make like I was interested in the bike he's sellin'."

"That sounds like a plan."

"There's just one thing though."

"What's that?"

"You'd hafta pretend to be my ole lady again."

That gave me pause. "What'd you say this guy's name was?"

"Rusty. Rusty Snyder."

"Okay, I've gotta take the dogs back to Jake's. Can you meet me there in forty-five minutes?"

"Sure thing." Jojo disconnected.

I chased the niggly feeling around for a few seconds and finally caught it. Why would this Loo rat out one of his own men? Could his feelings of outrage over Elsie's death outweigh loyalty to a fellow gang member?

Maybe Loo didn't like this guy for some reason. Then he might not have any qualms about turning him in.

,I shook my head and had a short debate with myself. I hadn't given it a thought when I'd ridden on Jojo's bike that short distance across A1A. But I wasn't totally comfortable with the idea of going with him by myself to who knew where to meet a Dark Demon biker named Rusty. If I followed in my car though, that would make no sense to this Rusty. Why would I tag along with "my old man" and not ride with him?

I needed a bodyguard, watching from afar. But I doubted Sergeant Phelps would approve of my independent investigation. Nor would Will, even if he wasn't two and a half hours away.

I placed a call and was surprised when Larry Merrick answered himself. I was expecting a secretary. After identifying myself, I asked, "Is this your cell?"

"Yup."

Okay, that explained it. "Hey, I hate to ask this of you in the middle of a work day but I need a hand with something. Jojo's got a lead on some guy."

"Oh, yeah. Who?"

"A Rusty Snyder. You know him?"

A half beat of silence. "Nope, can't say that the name rings any bells."

I told him about Jojo's plan for us to go look at the bike for sale.

"And you want me to follow discreetly," he said, "and make sure they behave themselves?"

"That's about it. He's meeting me at Jake's." I sucked in air, not sure what I'd do if he was too busy to help.

"Okay, I'll be there," he said. "But you probably won't see me."

I let out the pent-up air. "Thanks. I owe you one."

A low chuckle. "Never hurts to have a pretty woman beholdin' to you."

I chuckled a little too, out of politeness, but I wasn't sure how to take that comment.

At Jake and Janey's, I let the dogs out back and freshened their water dishes. Then I changed into jeans and my old tee-shirt again and pulled my hair back into a ponytail.

I grabbed the heavy denim jacket I'd thought to bring back with me from home. It was the closest thing I had to a winter coat. Leather would be better, but I figured Janey's too-big jackets would give it away that I was a novice...what?

Was there a name for women who sat on the back end of other people's bikes?

Jojo was on time and it looked like he'd made an effort to clean himself up some. Still I was glad there would be thick denim between me and his rather grungy-looking leather vest.

I pointed to his meaty, tattooed arms. "Don't you worry about road burn if you fall over?"

He stared at me, slowly shaking his head. "'Go down,' or 'drop the bike,'" he said with mild disgust. "Not 'fall over.'"

I nodded.

"Might be best if you keep your mouth shut as much as you can, at least 'bout bikes."

I nodded again, not at all offended. He was absolutely right. I did not know the lingo. "But I do need to try to get this Rusty talking about other things. How do I do that?"

"I'm gonna want to take the bike for a ride, see? And I wouldn't ride two up on an unfamiliar bike, 'specially one that ain't mine. So you stay back at Rusty's and get him talkin'. You can bring up the robberies directly. Everybody's buzzin' about 'em, cuz they like Izzy and Elsie."

"Sounds good."

"And honestly," Jojo added, "Rusty ain't the sharpest knife in the drawer, ya know what I mean?"

I hid a smile.

It took us a couple of minutes to get situated on the bike—again, I had trouble swinging my leg over his saddlebags—but eventually we were ready to go. He'd given me his only helmet, a dull black bowl-shaped thing. I was acutely aware of how it left half my brain exposed on the back of my head.

Jojo's shaggy hair was already blowing in my face as we roared out of the driveway. I had no chance to look around to see if Larry's SUV or motorcycle was nearby. I'd have to trust that he was with us.

Jojo turned onto A1A and for the next fifteen minutes I dug my fingers into the sides of his vest—yes, I touched it—and prayed. It took all of my willpower to keep from screaming as he wove in and out of cars and blew along straightaways. Larry had claimed that Jojo was basically law-abiding, but speed limits were apparently an exception to that concept.

I'd enjoyed riding behind Larry on his bike, but this was a whole other story.

Jojo suddenly slowed, plunging me forward against his back. Then he turned carefully onto a dirt road and progressed at a much more sedate speed down what appeared to be the main drag of a community made up of cement block cottages similar to my own, with a few derelict shacks and the occasional rusty house trailer scattered among them.

He pulled into the driveway of one such trailer and stopped the bike. "Get off," he said.

I awkwardly and gratefully clambered off the bike, almost falling in the dirt when my sneaker heel caught on the saddle bag.

Rusty Snyder, in nothing but faded jeans, a denim vest and black motorcycle boots, came out to meet us. He was even taller and thicker than Jake, a mountain of a man, with more ink than skin showing everywhere but the top of his shaved head, which was mercifully tattooless.

I don't object to tattoos in general, unless they're excessive, which these were. And ink where hair should be really gives me the creeps for some reason.

I immediately guessed the origins of his nickname, since his longish beard and mustache were the color of old bricks. Sweat trickled in rivulets down his muscular chest that was adorned with a phoenix rising from what looked like a fiery inferno. Funny, I always thought the fire was supposed to burn out before the legendary bird rose from the ashes.

"Hey, man." He smacked Jojo on the shoulder.

"This here's my ole lady." Jojo pointed vaguely in my direction. "Markie."

I was beginning to think his mangling of my name was because he couldn't remember it accurately, but now was not the time to correct him.

Rusty nodded my way, then gestured for us to follow him.

His garage was a corrugated steel building with a tin roof, twice the size of his house trailer. It was a few notches above Jojo's on the cleanliness scale. Although he had a fair amount of junk laying around, it seemed to be fairly organized.

If possible, it was hotter inside the building than out in the sun. But Rusty had several large fans set up, blowing air around the central area of the big space where he had been working. Several tools were scattered on the cement floor around a large bike that looked well used.

"I was just tunin' her up some," Rusty yelled over the whir of the fans.

Jojo walked all around it, nodding his head in a vaguely approving manner. Then he glanced around the building. "Where's your new one?" he said, also raising his voice.

"On order. Ain't come in yet," Rusty yelled back.

Jojo pointed to the bike between them. "Can I take 'er for a spin?"

"Sure." Rusty kicked tools and debris out of the way to create a path and Jojo mounted the bike, revved it up and rode it out of the open double doors where we'd entered.

Rusty made the follow-me gesture again and headed for another, smaller door in one corner.

I hesitated, but he wasn't even paying attention to whether or not I was following.

The door led to a grassy little oasis shaded by a stand of live oak trees a few yards away. I breathed a soft sigh of relief for multiple reasons. For one thing, it was ten degrees cooler here.

The roof of the building came out several feet, creating a porch of sorts, with wooden posts every few feet. Rusty went to an old refrigerator under the overhang and pulled out two bottles. He twisted off the caps and handed one to me.

I'm not much of a beer drinker and it was barely noon, but I smiled and took a big swig. It was icy cold and actually went down well.

He sucked down half of his bottle and burped. "How'd you end up with Jojo?"

"Mutual friend introduced us." It was the truth.

"Ain't you a bit outta his league, not to mention half his age?"

I took another sip of beer, smiled and said, "Yeah."

He laughed, a low deep rumble, and drained the rest of his beer. "Ya want another?"

"I'm good."

He chucked his empty in the general direction of a big metal tub already half full of bottles. Ignoring the clatter of glass against glass, he pulled another bottle out of the fridge.

"So, what's with this murder I've been hearin' about?" I said, attempting to sound the way Jojo's "ole lady" would probably talk. "Some pawn broker's wife. I thought I was movin' to this sleepy little beach town."

He shook his head, his broad cheeks pulled down in a sad expression. "Ain't right, what happened to Elsie. She and Izzie, they're good people, always helpin' out when they can." He turned half away from me, took a pull from his bottle.

"What do ya mean? You usually think of pawn brokers as kinda takin' advantage of folks."

"Nah." He turned back toward me. "Izzy took the pawned stuff mainly to help people out. Then he'd overprice it so nobody'd buy it, and you could redeem it later when you was flush again."

"Have you pawned things with him?"

"Sometimes. I tell him if it's somethin' I don't really care 'bout, so's he can go ahead and sell it. But if I don't say nothin', then he holds it for me."

"How does he make any money that way?"

"On the big-ticket stuff he gets at estate sales."

I nodded. "That makes sense."

He took another swig from his bottle. "Hey, help yerself to more beer. I gotta take a whiz." He took off for his trailer.

As soon as he was out of sight, I slipped back into the garage. It seemed the most likely hiding place for stolen treasure. I cruised once around the parameter, eyeballing piles of cardboard boxes stacked in the corners and a couple of wooden workbenches covered with random-shaped clumps of metal. I considered rummaging in the boxes, but the layers of dust on most of them indicated that any contraband they contained was probably stolen over a decade ago.

I wasn't real sure what I expected to find, but it wasn't long strips of shiny black metal—aluminum was my best guess. I reached out a hand to examine them further and a hard yank on my ponytail sent sharp pains zinging through my scalp.

A gruff voice said, "Whadaya think yer doin'?"

CHAPTER FOURTEEN

I whirled around, fists up, ready to defend myself—as if I knew how to do that.

Rusty stood behind me, hands in the air. "Whoa. Didn't mean ta hurt ya. But that metal, it can tear up your hands somethin' fierce."

I turned back partway and glanced at the black strips. "What are they for?"

"To make brackets and repair fenders and such. That's what I do, ya know, for a livin'." He sneered a little when he said the words *for a living.* "I fix people's bikes."

That would explain the random greasy items on the workbenches.

"Sorry. I didn't realize that metal was so sharp." I swallowed hard, still rattled some by the whole encounter. "Uh, thanks."

The roaring of a motorcycle engine announced Jojo's return. I blew out a quiet sigh.

We were about a half mile back down A1A when the beep-beep of a horn sounded behind us. Jojo moved his head slightly, glancing in his side view mirror.

The horn beeped again. I was too afraid of destabilizing the bike to look behind me—I'd been warned by both Larry and Jojo to not make any sudden moves.

Jojo swiveled his head to look back over his shoulder and I caught the side of a grin. "It's Bach," he yelled. He pulled into the next parking lot we came to, that of a convenience store, and came to a stop.

Larry pulled up next to us in his SUV. "You tryin' to steal my girl, Jojo?" he called out of his open window.

I was a little surprised by my reaction. I wasn't as irritated by the comment as I should have been.

"Nah." Jojo laughed. "We was just joy-ridin'."

"I'll take it from here," Larry said. "Thanks, man."

Jojo nodded and dismounted from the bike. He helped me off—my dang sneaker caught again. I thanked him and he gave me a mock salute, then jumped back on his bike and took off.

Larry had gotten out of his vehicle. He gestured toward it. "Milady, your chariot awaits."

I shook my head in mock disgust and climbed into the SUV. I was about to thank him for rescuing me from the rest of the harrowing ride on Jojo's bike.

But before I could open my mouth, he asked, "You had lunch?"

It seemed ungracious to decline the implied invitation. "No, and I'm starved."

My stomach rumbled but it also felt a bit queasy. Beer and an empty stomach are not a great combination.

A couple of minutes later, Larry pulled into the parking lot of a seafood restaurant on the ocean side of A1A. "This okay?"

I nodded enthusiastically.

We were seated at an outdoor table on the covered deck overlooking the water. A soft breeze blew off the ocean, making the heat bearable. I nabbed a packet of saltines from the basket of bread and crackers the waitress delivered after taking our orders.

"Don't know how helpful that little foray was," I said as I munched on the crackers, hoping they'd settle my stomach. "Yes, this guy Rusty's come into some money lately, in order to buy a new bike. But I didn't see any signs of stolen goods at his place."

"Did he seem nervous?" Larry said.

"Not at all. He was more than happy to ply me with beer at

eleven-forty-five and comment on how I was out of Jojo's league."

Larry smiled and then snorted. "Did he seem to think he *was* in your league?"

I grinned. "That was the implication."

"And is he?" Larry's eyes sparkled with humor.

I knew this was borderline flirting, but I was having fun. I tilted my head to one side, as if considering the question. "Well, his clothes were a little cleaner than Jojo's, but…" I shook my head. "Nah, too much ink."

Larry snickered. "What's he look like?"

I described Rusty, ending with, "His head is shaved smooth as a baby's bottom, but he's got this big, shaggy red beard."

Larry ran long, slender fingers through his wavy dark hair. "I've never quite understood the whole shaving-your-head thing."

I had the vague feeling that he was fishing for a compliment. I shifted a little in my seat and opted to change the subject. "How much does a new Harley cost?"

"What model?"

"He said it was top of the line."

"A lot then. At least twenty-five thousand, maybe more."

"Wow. I've never paid that much for a car."

The waitress brought our shared gator tail appetizer, with that tangy sauce on the side.

I had to be careful not to hog the deep-fried pieces of meat. Did I mention that I love gator tail?

"So, did you find out anything else interesting?" Larry asked.

I hastily finished chewing and grabbed my iced tea to wash the food down. *Ick!* The woman had brought me sweet tea.

"Not really." I was looking around for our waitress and only caught his expression out of the corner of my eye. His face seemed to relax as he stared at my profile.

Was he really falling for me, not just joking around with all the "my girl" stuff? Again, I wasn't as disturbed by the idea as I probably should've been.

I gave up on flagging down the waitress. I'd get her to change my tea when she brought our food.

"He seemed to care about the Belenkys, said Izzy helps people out by taking their stuff for pawn, but then overpricing it so it won't sell before they can claim it back."

The corners of Larry's mouth pulled down. "I didn't know that, but it explains some of his prices."

"Hey, thanks for following along. I hated to take you away from your work."

He shrugged. "My workload tends to ebb and flow, and frankly I'm getting kind of bored with it all."

"Hmm, you're a little young to be burning out already."

"Not sure it's burnout. Probably more that I picked the wrong profession to begin with. I was focused on the money lawyers make and didn't give much thought to whether or not I'd like it."

No wonder he was willing to get in on the excitement of investigating. "How's the personal injury stuff going? Isn't that more interesting?"

He shrugged again. "Not really. But I'm working on retiring young. Or maybe I'll marry a rich woman." He winked at me. "How much money do dog trainers make?"

I rolled my eyes and we laughed. He gestured for me to take the last chunk of gator tail.

I wanted to be polite and give it to him, but I was too greedy. I gobbled it down and reached for my napkin.

"Seriously," Larry said, "I would like to get to know you better. I know you said you're involved but how, um, intense is that involvement?"

I covered my hesitation by patting my lips again with the napkin. "Pretty intense."

"You're not interested in pursuing other possibilities?"

"No, but I'm flattered." The words were fine—firm but tinged with regret, but I felt heat creeping up my cheeks. I wished I could hide under the table. Maybe a quick trip to the ladies' room?

Miraculously, the waitress arrived with two platters heaped with fried shrimp and fries. I explained about the tea issue, she apologized and swept off with my glass. And by the time all that was done, my face had returned to its normal temperature.

"I really appreciate your help with the case," I said.

He waved a hand in the air. "And that'll keep coming. I'm not just helping out to get in good with you. I don't want Jake and Janey to suffer for something they didn't do."

We ate in reasonably companionable silence for a few minutes. Then he said, "So, you don't think this Rusty is our guy?"

"I doubt it. He looks pretty scary, but I think he's basically harmless."

We chatted about other things as we finished our meal.

"Oh, almost forgot," Larry said. "I think I might have a solution to the not-for-profit selling you the dog."

"Really?" I smiled. "I wasn't going to mention it. Figured it was too soon for you to have anything for me." Then I held my breath and prayed.

"They can't sell you the dog, because that could be construed as making a profit. Nor can they give him to you because you're not an injured veteran."

"Our recipients have PTSD mainly," I interjected, then realized I shouldn't have, since that indirectly gave him private information about Jake.

But Larry went on, so maybe he hadn't taken notice of what I'd said.

"What I think they can do is trade one trained dog for another. As you said, the IRS views these animals as assets, interchangeable assets. So you give them a trained dog for free and you get Buddy."

I felt giddy with relief. "Wow. Would that mean I'd get back the money I've already paid them toward him?"

It would definitely mean I'd be training two dogs at once this fall.

"Yeah, but don't get too excited yet. I still need to research a few things, to make sure we're on solid ground. Then I can write a contract up for you and the agency to sign. If you want me to, that is?"

"How much would that cost?"

He waved his hand. "No charge."

"Uh, I can't let you do that. And besides the agency may be willing to pay for it, or at least split the cost with me. I need to call Mattie either way, before you write up the contract."

"Sure."

The waitress brought the check. I made a grab for it, but Larry got to it first. "I invited you, remember?" He grinned. "And now you owe me even more."

I laughed a nervous laugh. I wasn't sure where he was going with that.

We were back at Jake's before I found out. I thanked him again for his help and for lunch and opened my door to climb out of the SUV.

He touched my forearm, and when I turned back, his lips landed on mine.

It was a sweet kiss, not passionate, but it sent tingles through my system. I pulled back.

"Now we're even for the first IOU," he said with a grin. "I'll collect on the other one some other time."

He let go of my arm and I got the heck out of there quick, my emotions all jumbled up in my chest. The primary one being guilt, because I'd felt more flattered than annoyed by the kiss.

I opted to ignore the situation with Larry—I do a great ostrich impersonation—and focus on the case. I only had a day and half that I could afford to spend on it.

After checking on the dogs and their water dishes, I changed into something cooler and less biker chick to go talk to Izzy Belenky.

I debated about taking Buddy with me. His big body and wagging tail might be a problem in the pawn shop. I was going to leave him, but changed my mind at the last minute. Larry might think he had an answer to the tax dilemma, but I was still feeling like a clingy mama.

"Come on, boy."

Felix started to follow. "Sorry," I said and gave him the hand signal to lie down. He settled onto his belly in the middle of living room and watched us leave with those soulful eyes of his.

The significance of the sign sank in this time. *Belenky's Fine Jewelry and Collectibles* in big gold letters, *Pawn Broker* in smaller black ones.

I pushed open the door and blew out the breath I hadn't realized I'd been holding. The broken glass was gone of course, and everything else was as neat as a pin. Long rows of glass-enclosed display cases ran the length of the shop. Amongst the larger items to one side was a cello that I was pretty sure hadn't been there before.

I averted my eyes. My ex-husband had left me for a cello player. Although I'd long since decided I was better off without him, cellos were still a symbol of all things evil to me.

Izzy Belenky bustled through a door at the back of the shop and stood behind the counter. With Buddy in tow, I approached slowly, recalling all too vividly what I'd found behind that counter last time I'd been here.

I was pretty sure Izzy was standing right where his wife's bleeding head had been, but then maybe he didn't know that. He probably hadn't seen her here, but rather at the morgue.

I shuddered.

Now I had two places I couldn't look, so I focused on Izzy's face. He was a roly-poly man but today his cheeks were almost sunken. And his eyes were haunted, despite the smile he'd plastered on. "How can I help you, miss?"

Crapola. He doesn't recognize me.

The good news was he hadn't reacted negatively to having a dog in his store. I signaled for Buddy to lie down and he complied.

"I, um, was the one who was here, you know, that day... of the last robbery."

Izzy's face sagged as recognition dawned. "Yes. Ms. Banks,

isn't it? What can I do for you?"

I was realizing I should have thought this out better ahead of time. "Uh, I wanted to ask you about a few things."

He narrowed his eyes slightly. "Such as?"

My brain cast about, and landed on diamonds. "You said something about diamonds last time we talked. That the thieves had gotten the diamonds. What did you mean?"

He sighed. "I'd just bought them, from the estate of a jewelry maker over in Orlando, along with a bunch of his other stuff. Mostly tools that I probably won't be able to sell. But the gems were worth it."

"And the thieves took them. Where did you have them?"

"In the safe, in the back. They must've…" He trailed off, his eyes suddenly shiny with tears.

"They made your wife open it?" I said gently.

He nodded, swallowed hard.

"What did they take the other time they were here?"

"Gold rings and some silver jewelry, from another estate sale. Some very nice things." He gestured toward one of the display cases. "They were in there. I was here by myself and those two came in, with a gun, said to open the case or else."

"That's all they took?"

"Yes. They went right to that case. Looked in, then the guy pulled his gun. I'd only had them a few days."

"The rings," I clarified.

He nodded again. "Some of them were quite beautiful, and unique," he said wistfully. "One I'd been tempted to keep for myself. It had little gold snakes winding up and around the stone." He sketched a winding pattern with his index finger on the glass counter top. "A large black opal."

I suppressed a shudder. Gold snakes wouldn't be my preference, but I got it that this man truly loved jewelry—for its own sake. He wore little of it himself, only his wedding ring and a thin silver chain with a small star of David on it. But maybe that was only here at the shop, to avoid tempting robbers any more than the cases full of valuables already did.

He leaned forward, his elbows on the counter. "The police think somebody's been casing the place, keeping an eye out for small expensive stuff that they can carry away in their pockets. Say, why are you interested in all this?"

Here it was, the moment of reckoning.

"I'm dog and house-sitting for the Blacks. I know them because I trained Jake's dog, Felix."

"I know Felix," Izzie said. "He's a good boy, real well-behaved."

"Thank you." I let out my pent-up breath. So far, so good.

He leaned even further forward and looked down at Buddy. "That your dog?"

Duh! snarky me thought. In my mind's eye, I slapped a hand over her mouth.

"Yes, and he's my mentor dog. I use him to help train the others."

Izzy smiled for the first time. "Hey, boy."

Buddy looked up, but he stayed on the floor.

"It's okay, boy," I said.

He stood and wagged his tail.

"I'm having trouble seeing Jake and Janey as thieves." I once again held my breath.

Izzie shook his head slowly. "I did too, at first. I didn't even think of them when I was describing those two to the deputies. But then one of the detectives came back later and said they had witnesses who saw them getting on their bikes and taking off. And the bikes are kind of distinctive, from what they said. I don't know one motorcycle from another myself."

"You didn't see them getting away?"

"I ran out the door, but then I stopped on the sidewalk. I knew I couldn't catch them, and I needed to call the police."

"You don't have an alarm?"

"Yes, a silent one. But I like to call 911 myself as well. Sometimes I'm faster than the alarm company."

"Sounds like you've gotten robbed a lot."

He shrugged. "Not as much as most pawn brokers. I try to cultivate a good relationship with the community, even those who are down and out."

"You've succeeded. Everybody speaks highly of you."

He managed a small smile. "So, are you a detective or something?"

"No, just trying to help out." I quickly added, "What did you see from the door?"

"The rear ends of their bikes. The black one skidded and went down, but the big guy jumped up and got right back on."

"And the woman was on a red trike?"

"Yes, one of those three-wheeled jobs."

"I know you described them for the police, but could you tell me what they were wearing and all?"

"Hang on. I got a copy of the statement I gave the police that time." He stepped back through the door into his backroom and came out a few seconds later with a manila file folder.

I caught a glimpse of the label—*Robbery, Sept. 8, 2016*. The first robbery, last Thursday.

"Gotta keep everything organized for the insurance company." He walked over to a computer printer on a small table behind the counter and lifted the lid. "I'll make you a copy."

"That's great." I couldn't believe my luck that he was cooperating. If it had been my spouse who'd been killed… My throat tightened. I shoved aside images of this poor man's wife lying behind the counter.

He came back over and handed me two sheets of paper.

"Thanks." I folded them and stuck them in my pocket to read later. "What made you think it was Jake and Janey?" I'd already kind of asked that question, but I wanted to see what he'd say this time.

He lifted one shoulder in a half shrug. "I'm not totally convinced it was them. They're about the right height and weight, but I couldn't see nothing of the robbers' faces. They had their helmets on, and ski masks covering their faces. He was all in black—jeans, jacket, gloves. I saw her hands. They were pale white. And there were wisps of blonde hair sticking out under her helmet."

He stopped, took a deep breath. "The timing, though, that's hard to ignore. I get robbed twice, then they get arrested. No more robberies until they're out on bail. Then no more again once they're back in jail."

"Wait! You got robbed twice before this last one?"

"The police think the first one was more a dry run. Same guy, but by himself. Walks up to the front, pulls his hand out from behind him and he's got a big rock in it. Smashed the top out of one of the cases. Grabs a bunch of jewelry and runs out."

"Did you follow him?"

"Yes, but I was also trying to call the police on my phone at the same time. He disappeared in between the rows of cars, then I hear a motorcycle revving up as I'm on the phone. Saw him swing out onto A1A and take off."

"You were here by yourself that time too?"

"Yes. It's always been between twelve and twelve-thirty, which is when Elsie and me..." He stopped, swiped a hand across his eyes, then cleared his throat. "One of us would go out to get our lunches around then. We should've changed that routine after the second robbery, but... Well, the detectives seemed so sure it was Jake and Janey. And we certainly didn't think they'd rob us again, when they were out on bail." His voice went up some in pitch.

That was indeed a shocker in my mind too, that the thieves were so brazen to come back that last time. But then again, diamonds were quite the incentive, especially when you had a good scapegoat to take the blame.

"I talked to some folks here in the shopping center. They said the woman walked or ran funny." I intentionally didn't get specific, to see what he'd do with it.

He tilted his head, reminding me of Buddy's patented look. "Don't remember that, but the guy limped."

I felt my eyebrows go up despite my best efforts to maintain my cool. "Really? Which leg did he favor?"

Izzie came around the counter and demonstrated, rocking a little from side to side as he walked down an aisle, favoring his left leg.

"That's very interesting," I said. "Thanks for all your help, Mr. Belenky."

"Izzy," he corrected, then narrowed his eyes at me. "You really don't think the Blacks did it?"

I answered his question with another one of my own. "Have you ever seen Jake Black limp?"

CHAPTER FIFTEEN

Will's unmarked sedan was parked in Jake's driveway when I got there. My heart skipped a beat, then sped up, and I could feel a smile spreading across my face.

I spotted his tall, lean body propped against the railing of the front porch and warmth filled my chest.

I pulled in behind his car and could hardly contain myself as I released Buddy from his safety strap. Then we ran along the walk to the porch.

Will grabbed me up in a bear hug.

I breathed him in—the starched cotton scent of his uniform shirt, his woodsy aftershave, and a hint of male sweat—and felt myself relax like I hadn't in days.

My stomach twisted. Why had I ever let Larry Merrick kiss me?

Then Will was kissing me and the heat exploding inside of me was like a ballistic missile compared to the little firecrackers I'd felt from what's-his-name's kiss.

Will finally let me go. Gasping a little, I said, "How'd you get off so early?"

"Decided to ignore the paperwork. I missed you."

"Me too, missed you that is." The smile I gave him was a little forced because most of my emotional energy was going into tamping down guilt feelings about Larry. After all, I hadn't kissed him. *He'd* kissed me.

Heat rising in my cheeks, I turned my back to Will and

fumbled with my keys as I tried to unlock the front door.

Will leaned over and greeted Buddy with an ear scratch.

My heart swelled in my chest. One of the things I loved about this man was that he always paid attention to my dogs.

As I pushed the door open, I vowed to set Larry straight, if he tried to flirt or kiss me again.

Felix was standing in the middle of the living room, his forlorn eyes glued to the entranceway. I crouched down and hugged his neck. "Sorry, boy," I whispered. He turned his jowly head toward me and gave me a soulful look.

My throat aching, I took the dogs out back for a bathroom break.

Then I retrieved a beer for Will and a bottle of water for myself from the fridge. We settled on the sofa, his arm loosely around my shoulders.

Suddenly I wanted to tell him everything and have *him* help me solve the riddle. Felix needed his family back, and I felt like I was on the verge of an aha moment.

I sat up some and turned to face Will. "Look, I've only got tonight and tomorrow to help Jake and Janey. Then I've got to go home and get back to training dogs. So can I run some stuff by you?"

He looked a little startled and opened his mouth.

I braced myself for the why-aren't-you-letting-this-go lecture.

But he closed his mouth again. Then he said, "Sure."

A bit disoriented by his easy acquiescence, I filled him in on most of it—leaving the trip to the bikers' bar and Mr. Gruff Voice out. I ended with Jojo's and my visit to Rusty's garage that morning and then my conversation with Izzie Belenky.

By the time I was done, the furrow in his brow was as deep as a canyon.

"What the heck do you think you're doing, Marcia? You're gonna get yourself killed."

I bristled. That was the reaction I'd initially expected but not the one I'd fantasized in my mind.

I crossed my arms over my chest. "Here's the deal, Will Haines. I'm going to help my friends out of this mess with or without you. If you're so worried about my safety, then help me figure out what's going on."

My mouth fell open. *Where the heck did that come from?*

Will had the slightly startled look on his face again. "Okay."

Did he just say okay?

I pressed my advantage and handed over the copy of Izzy's statement. I'd skimmed it in the parking lot before heading home, but hadn't seen anything that Izzy hadn't told me. Maybe Will would catch something I'd missed.

When he'd finished reading and looked up, I said, "So you're the law enforcement officer, what do you make of all that?"

"Jake doesn't limp," he said in a clarifying tone.

"Nope, and the way Izzie was walking, that would actually throw Jake off balance. He..." How to explain it?

"His legs work fine. It's the balance center inside his brain that was injured." I patted the back of my head where that balance center is located, if I was recalling my neurobiology correctly. "He can go along for hundreds of feet or yards, walking perfectly okay, and then suddenly he'll wobble and lose his balance."

I jumped up. "Let me show you."

I got Felix's service vest and put it on him. The dog gazed up at me, his big eyes expectant. Together we demonstrated, with me walking normally and then faking a wobble, and Felix bracing himself as I grabbed for the bar on his vest.

Will nodded.

I removed the vest and gave the dog the release signal. He trotted over to lie down beside Buddy.

"You got anything else?" Will actually sounded like a police officer conferring with a colleague.

My chest warmed as I returned to the sofa. "Yeah." I told him about the other witnesses who'd reported that the woman had held her belly as she'd run.

"So?" he said.

"Have you ever seen a chubby woman, say Janey Black's size, run? Does she hold her stomach?"

He seemed to give that some thought. "I see what you mean. You think she was wearing padding and that's what she was holding on to?"

"Yup." Then I took a deep breath and asked, "So where do I go from here?"

His hesitation was slight. Then he leaned forward and ticked off fingers on his left hand with his right. "First, re-interview some of the people at the shopping center and ask about how the guy walked or ran. Keep your questions neutral so you're not leading the witnesses. Then talk to this Jojo again about the biker outlaw gang. Oh, and check out his record and Rusty's, and while you're at it, check out that lawyer, Merrick."

"Larry? You think he has a record?" Talking about the guy I'd had an illicit kiss with was making my insides feel funny and not in a good way.

"No." Will sat back and dropped his arm around me again. "But you cover all the bases."

I told my insides to settle down and leaned back into the circle of his arm. "I don't have access to people's police records."

Will stiffened slightly, but then he sighed. "I'll do those background checks tomorrow. Any news on the Buddy issue?"

"Yes, but that reminds me. Let me call Mattie first, before it gets too late." I made the call and when she answered, I filled her in on Larry's idea. Listening to my end of the conversation, Will smiled and nodded.

"Don't get your hopes up yet," I whispered to him. "He doesn't know for sure it'll work."

"I like it," Mattie was saying in my ear. "If this lawyer decides it'll work, tell him to go ahead and write up the papers."

"Thank you, Mattie," I said in relief. "Uh, do you think the board would agree to split the cost of his fee with me?"

Silence for half a beat. "They'll pay the whole fee, Marcia. *You* didn't do anything wrong here." Her tone was emphatic.

I thanked her again and disconnected.

Will was grinning from ear to ear. "So you're not going to lose Buddy. Let's go out to dinner to celebrate."

"Celebrating may be premature. And I had a big lunch. I'd rather just forage in the kitchen later, if you don't mind."

Will's face fell some. "Then what *do* you want to do this evening?"

I gave him an impish grin. "I have a few things in mind."

I was humming to myself as I drove to the strip shopping center the next morning, enjoying the afterglow of a wonderful evening with Will.

At least he didn't bring up the subject of kids this time, my snarky inner voice said.

"Shut up," I said out loud.

Buddy, hooked to his safety strap in the backseat, cocked his head.

I made eye contact with him in the rearview mirror. "It's all good, boy."

His tail thumped against the seat.

A few butterflies of anxiety still fluttered in my chest, but I was trying to convince myself that Larry's plan would work. And Mattie was pleased with it, which was more than half the battle where the agency was concerned. She could usually talk the board of directors into doing whatever she wanted.

Again, I felt a bit guilty about the service dog vest Buddy was wearing—especially since one of my pet peeves is how easy it is to get service animal status in Florida—but I couldn't bear to leave him behind today.

We re-visited all of the folks at the shopping center who'd witnessed the thieves making their escape. Based on Will's advice, I carefully worded my questions. "Did you notice anything unusual about the man's gait?" They all shook their heads and said no, he'd ran like a totally able-bodied person, or words to that effect. I wrote down all their names this time and which store they owned or worked for.

It's very helpful to have a sheriff for a boyfriend when playing Nancy Drew.

I believed Izzy was telling the truth, but these other witnesses' contradictory reports also pointed away from Jake. It was unlikely that he'd run at all since running was likely to throw him off balance. I concluded that the robber didn't know Jake, or at least had never seen him walk any distance, and he knew little or nothing about traumatic brain injury.

By the time I was finished with the interviews, I was hungry, having skipped breakfast. Since Will and I had depleted the Blacks' lunchmeat, cheese and bread supply the previous evening, I decided to stop in Publix before heading back.

"Plastic okay?" the young African-American bagger smiled at me. His features suggested that he had Downs' Syndrome.

I nodded.

"Is that a service dog?" he asked.

"Yes." I resisted the urge to explain the whole mentor dog thing, figuring that would just be confusing.

"Mr. Jake has a service dog," he said.

"Yes, he does. He's a friend of mine."

"Really?" The young man beamed as he stuffed my purchases into a plastic bag.

"Fifteen-sixty," the female cashier said.

I handed over a twenty and got my change.

"May I help you out with that?" the young man said, following the script he'd been taught, even though my purchases barely filled one plastic bag.

"Yes," I said.

He beamed some more and took charge of my cart.

I followed him out into the parking lot, then moved up beside him. "So, you know Mr. Jake?"

He nodded. "He lets me pet Felix. I'm the only one who can do that, once we're out here."

I almost laughed out loud, at the same time as my throat

closed. It was so like Jake to take the time to release Felix and let this young man pet him.

"What's your name?" I asked.

"Derek."

"So, Derek, have you ever seen Mr. Jake walk funny?"

He gave me a long soul-searching look. "Whadda you mean?"

Hmm, vagueness apparently wasn't going to work here. "Does he do this?" I imitated a limp, intentionally favoring my right side rather than the left.

Derek shook his head. "No. He lets me pet his dog."

Eyes stinging a little, I thanked him for his help as he put my measly one bag of groceries in my car.

Then I gave Buddy the release signal so Derek could pet him.

My phone rang as I was driving home. The number on the Bluetooth screen seemed vaguely familiar but no name was attached to it, so it wasn't someone in my contacts. I didn't answer.

Good thing I didn't, because when I got to Jake's house and checked voicemail, there was another message from Mr. Gruff Voice.

"Curiosity killed the cat, you know. It can do the same to dogs."

CHAPTER SIXTEEN

With trembling fingers, I found Sergeant Phelps's number in my contacts and punched his name. The phone rang twice.

"Yeah."

"Hi, it's Marcia Banks."

"I know." He didn't sound all that surprised nor happy to be hearing from me.

"I need to report some threatening calls. They're related to the Blacks' case."

"What?" He sounded slightly less hostile.

I told him about Mr. Gruff Voice, who was probably related to Mr. Leather Jacket Sleeve.

"Bring me your phone, but don't come inside the building. Call me when you're in the parking lot."

"When?"

"Now would be good." He disconnected.

I had a short debate with myself. I really wanted to take the dogs with me, to make sure they were safe, but I also wanted to see Jake while I was at the sheriff's department. I was seriously considering giving him what I had and then getting out of Dodge.

I opted for the latter plan, since I also needed to find out what I should do about Felix when I left tomorrow. Or maybe I'd leave tonight.

I set the house alarm—something I hadn't been doing during the day, for fear I would accidentally set it off when I came back in—and headed for the sheriff's office by myself.

Will called before I'd even gotten to A1A. "Got some info for you," he said cheerfully.

"Great," I said, trying to keep the butterflies in my stomach and chest from showing up in my voice. I wasn't sure I was ready to tell him about the threats. He'd either drop everything in his own life, including his reelection campaign, to come protect me, or he'd demand I leave Buckland Beach this very minute. Either way, we'd fight and my nerves weren't up to dealing with that right now.

"Joseph Johnson's record is surprisingly clean," Will was saying, "only a few traffic violations, mostly speeding. But your lawyer buddy, Merrick, he has a juvie record that's sealed."

The butterflies kicked up quite a ruckus at the words *lawyer buddy*. I wanted to protest that he wasn't my buddy, but for once, I was able to rein in my tongue. Such a comment would most likely make Will wonder why she doth protest too much.

"Nothing as an adult, except again a few speeding tickets."

"Wouldn't something serious in Larry's background keep him from being a lawyer?"

"Probably not if it was when he was a kid. An adult felony might matter though. I don't know. Not sure how that works with the bar association. By the way, he's a native of Buckland Beach."

"So Jojo's clean," I said. "That's kind of surprising."

"Yeah, a little. He may hang out with that Dark Demons gang, but he hasn't been involved in any of their illegal activities, or at least he hasn't gotten caught."

Of course Will would add that last part, skeptical lawman that he was.

"He's a retired plumber," he said, "from Milwaukee. A widower. Wife died of cancer five years ago, and he moved down here."

"What about Rusty?" I pulled up to the stop sign at A1A.

"He's from New York originally, but he's lived in half a dozen states. His record's not so clean, but nothing worse than speeding tickets and drunk and disorderlies. Lots of them. At least, that's all that's stuck. He's been charged with other things, including robbery, but the charges were dropped for insufficient evidence. Once was for vehicular manslaughter. His story was that he saw another biker go off the road and he stopped to help, but the prosecutor and the sheriff were skeptical because the dead guy in the ditch was from a rival gang."

"There's another outlaw biker gang in Florida?" Finally a gap in traffic. I made the turn onto A1A.

"Yup, in South Florida. They don't usually come up this far, but of course they have to come through central Florida if they're headed out of state. The dead guy's buddies said he was going to Georgia to visit his mother."

Driving slowly in the lunchtime traffic, I digested the information Will had given me. "Did you find out anything more about Detective Wright?"

"No. The guy I know on the Jersey force said he hadn't heard anything about it." A slight pause. "But I think he might be stonewalling me."

"Hmm, that smells of a cover-up."

"Or just brothers in blue protecting each other's reputations."

"But wouldn't he consider you a brother in blue also?" Even though technically Will's uniform was khaki.

"Apparently not. Now that I'm a sheriff, I guess I fall into the 'brass' category." His voice sounded wistful. "Hey, have you talked to Pete recently? When can you go home?"

I suspected his motives had less to do with me being somewhat closer geographically and more to do with wanting me to stop investigating.

"I'll call him in a while," I said. "Maybe I can sleep in my own bed tonight."

A low chuckle. "And maybe I can join you there?"

I actually grinned at the Bluetooth screen with Will's name on it. "Maybe," I teased, "if you're a good boy."

Another low chuckle. "Keep me posted. Love you." And he was gone.

The flirting with Will had distracted my butterflies but now that I was turning into the sheriff department's parking lot, they stirred again.

I called the sergeant.

"Be right there." He was definitely a man of few words.

Thirty seconds later, he stepped out the front door, looked around, then sauntered toward my car. I clicked the locks open.

He settled his bulk into my passenger seat. "You got your phone?"

"Yes, but I can't just turn it over to you. I need it."

He narrowed his eyes at me. "Lemme hear the messages."

I found them in my voicemail and played the first one on speaker, then the second one.

He nodded slightly and dug a small pad and pen out of his shirt pocket. "Gimme the guy's phone number."

I read it off from missed calls. "Do you have to take the phone?"

He frowned. "Not yet, but be careful not to erase those messages. Lemme check the number and see who it leads back to."

"Thanks." I gave him a smile, trying to warm him up some. But he seemed resistant to warming, even on a hot day like today.

"And someone accosted you in the Cracker Barrel?" he asked.

"Yeah, it all happened really quick." I described the assault to him as he jotted notes on his pad.

"You hurt?" he asked, glancing sideways at me.

I shook my head.

He returned his pad and pen to his shirt pocket. "Was thinking about giving you another lead, but now... You better let this be."

I was curious, despite my vow to turn everything over to Jake's lawyer and be done with it.

"What lead? And why have you been feeding me these leads instead of checking them out yourself?"

Sergeant Phelps turned his head and scowled at me. Sitting this close in the car, the bushy eyebrows coming together over hard eyes were pretty intimidating. I was glad we were on the same side, sort of.

"I was taken off the case," he said, "'cause Jake's a friend of mine."

Which told me two things. One, the sheriff might just fire him if she found out he was feeding me leads, and two, he cared enough about Jake and Janey to take that risk.

"So, what's this other lead? I'm just curious. I'm not going to do anything with it."

He pointed to the phone. "You got a short memory about curiosity, doncha?"

With effort, I maintained eye contact, without saying anything—mostly because I didn't know what else to say.

He sighed. "All the focus has been on Jake's bike 'cause it's so distinctive. They haven't checked out who else might own, or maybe borrowed, a red Honda Goldwing trike. That's a pretty distinctive-looking bike too and not extremely common."

"Where would one start to look into it? Even though I'm not going to."

He closed his eyes for a second and shook his head.

"Did your lab find anything interesting on Jake's bike?" I was asking as much to keep him engaged as anything else.

He seemed to hesitate, but then he answered, "Sand in the scratches on the saddlebag matched what was on the parking lot entrance where the robber's bike went down."

My heart sank. No wonder the sheriff was convinced they had the right culprits.

"Otherwise it was clean." Phelps rubbed his face, then added in a mumble. "Too clean."

"As in no fingerprints?"

He nodded.

"Then somebody wiped it down after they traded the saddlebags."

"We've only got Jake's word that those bags aren't his, and yeah, somebody could've wiped the bike, or maybe Jake had cleaned it recently. You saw how neat his garage was. He's a tad compulsive that way."

"But even if he'd cleaned the bike," I said, "there should be some prints. He'd probably move it out into the center of the garage to clean it, wouldn't he?"

The sergeant grunted. "Or out in the driveway even."

"So there would be prints on the handlebars at least, from when he put it back."

"I'm not the one who needs convincing of that." He opened the passenger door. "Stay outta trouble. I'll be in touch."

I rooted in my purse for something to write on, found an old grocery list and turned it over, then retrieved a pen. I made a quick list of all the things I'd found out, afraid I'd forget something while talking to Jake.

A few minutes later, I was reading that list to Jake via the phone line in the jail's visitation room.

"Geez, Marcia," he said into his receiver, "you've dug up more stuff than that fancy investigator my lawyer hired. Speaking of which, would you mind calling him and giving all that to him. I might not remember it all."

"Of course. Are you still having memory problems?"

He paused, his cheeks flushing a little. "Not as much, but yeah, especially when I'm stressed out."

I couldn't even begin to imagine how stressful being locked up was for him, and with no Felix to help with the anxiety.

"Are you doing okay with balance issues?"

He snorted softly. "Yeah, they've got me in a cell by myself that's about six by six. There's always a wall within reach."

"Isn't there any way your lawyer can get you out on bail?"

"He's working on a deal with house arrest. Janey and I'd have to wear ankle monitors."

"That would be so much better." But I couldn't help wondering what they'd do for groceries and such. Maybe Publix would deliver.

"Unfortunately, I have to leave either tonight or tomorrow,"

I told him. "I've got to get back to my training."

"That's fine, Marcia. You've already been such a big help. If you don't hear from us before you have to go, call our lawyer. He can let you know if we're close to getting out of here. If not, I guess it would be best if you took Felix with you. Would that be a problem?"

"No, that's fine. I can bring him back to you when you do get out. You mind if I take his crate as well?"

"No problem. It's in our bedroom." He gave me the lawyer's phone number, which I wrote in the margin of my list.

"Take care, Jake," I said.

"I'm trying." He gave me a small smile as he hung up the phone on his side of the glass barrier. Then as he pushed to a stand, he lost his balance and had to grab for the edge of the metal counter.

I quickly turned away, hoping he'd believe that I hadn't seen his moment of weakness.

"Hey, what're you doing?" the guard by the door barked at him. I could hear him clearly through the glass.

Jake held up his hands. "Nothin'," he called over. "Stood up too fast, that's all."

I moved toward the exit, but watched out of the corner of my eye. Jake walked stiffly and carefully toward the door on his side. As he passed the guard, the man put his hand on Jake's shoulder and gave him a shove.

Jake careened into the wall. He grabbed for the doorjamb with one hand, but his other fist was clenched and his face was turning red.

"Jake, no!" I yelled.

Both he and the guard turned to look at me. The guard glared. "Lady, your visit is over. You need to leave."

Not hardly, bozo. Hands on hips, I stared him down until Jake had walked out of the room. Through the momentarily open doorway, I caught sight of part of another guard's uniform and breathed out a small sigh. The obnoxious guard was not the one who would be escorting Jake back to his cell.

As I left via the visitors' door, I was shaking like a leaf—one part fear for Jake, one part anger. Instead of going out the jail exit, I turned right into a hallway that I thought would lead me back to the main reception area of the sheriff's department. I was going to report that guard before he had a chance to retaliate against Jake.

Unfortunately, I ran into Detective Wright, almost literally. I stopped a few inches short of colliding with his chest.

He stepped back. "What are you doing here?" His tone was not friendly.

"You all need to check your ventilation system," snarky me snapped at him, "'cause obviously your brains aren't getting enough oxygen."

"What the devil do you mean by that?" His hands were on his hips, reminiscent of my recent stance.

I wrestled control away from Ms. Snarky. "Sorry, I just had a run-in with one of your jail guards."

Wright snorted. "I can't imagine that you did anything to provoke him."

"Actually, I didn't. I kept him from abusing a prisoner." My voice rose, drawing attention from several uniformed deputies down the hall. "Mr. Black, to be exact. A war hero who has TBI and cannot afford to be knocked around."

The uniforms headed our way. Wright held out a hand toward them in a stop gesture.

"Keep your voice down," he said to me. "What happened?"

I told him.

"I'll look into it," he said in a clipped tone. Then he took me firmly by the elbow and escorted me to the jail exit.

I somehow made it across the parking lot to my car, despite the fact that my legs had turned to jelly. I may put up a good snarky front, but in truth, I hate confrontation.

I locked myself in, turned the key and ramped the AC way up. I gulped the chill air coming out of the vents until my heart rate returned to normal.

I was wavering on the get out of Dodge decision.

Even before the guard incident, I'd been concerned about Jake's mood. Despite his excitement over my discoveries, there'd been an undertone of depression in his voice. Not too surprising, considering he was an unwilling guest of Buckland County.

His situation was way too reminiscent of another client's, who'd been accused of murdering his wife. That had not ended well for the client.

I felt queasy. Could I live with myself if I turned my back on Jake and he suffered a similar fate?

Then I remembered Mr. Gruff Voice's threat against Buddy and Felix. Part of me wanted to call the lawyer right now, from the jail's parking lot, and turn over everything, then go back to the Blacks' and pack my things.

I opted to put off the decision and the call to Jake's lawyer until I got to the house. I was anxious to check on the dogs.

As I pulled out of the parking lot onto A1A, my phone rang. My dashboard screen informed me it was Pete.

"Hey, Marcia, a slight delay…" Static garbled his next words.

Now what?

"How slight, Pete?" I didn't bother to keep my annoyance out of my voice.

"Not too bad. Another half a day. Should be done by tomorrow noon at the latest."

"What's the delay? More problems with the roof?"

"Nothing major…" Again his words were scrambled.

"Look, we've got a lousy connection and I'm driving. I'll call you back later."

More static and a faint "Okay."

I disconnected the call, then glanced up in my rearview mirror. Some jerk in a big white pickup was right on my tail. I looked at my speedometer. No wonder. The speed limit along this section of A1A was ridiculously low but I'd managed to drop below even that while distracted by the phone call.

I nudged my accelerator and got my speed up to the limit.

But this didn't seem to satisfy the driver of the truck. He was still right on my back bumper.

I sped up a bit more, five miles over the limit. Still on my bumper.

I wasn't in the mood for a ticket, on top of all my other expenses, so I pulled into the next parking lot entrance I came to, intending to let this jerk go on by.

But he followed me in and then tailed me as I circled the parking lot, intending to return to the entrance.

What the heck? Adrenaline jolted through my system. Was I about to be a victim of road rage?

Should I park and go in the building? I glanced in that direction. It was a bar and grill, maybe two steps above the biker hangout I'd gone to with Jojo. And the parking lot was pretty crowded, mostly with pickup trucks, about half of them white.

Heart pounding, I accelerated as much as I could in such tight quarters and raced for the exit. Waiting for a break in the traffic, I looked in the mirror again. For a disorienting moment, I wasn't sure what I was seeing. Then the meaning of the image registered in my brain.

The driver of the truck was wearing a ski mask. In Florida. In September.

I roared out into a too-small opening in the traffic and floored it. Unfortunately, I quickly caught up with the car in front of me and had to slow to the speed limit again.

I stared at the rearview mirror and finally made out the white pickup four vehicles back. Or *a* white pickup. It might or might not be the same one.

I ran through a yellow light and then took the next right, heading away from the ocean. I made several random turns, watching the mirror more than the road.

No sign of a white truck after a couple of miles. Air whooshed out of my lungs and my body sagged in my seat.

There was only one problem. I was out in the countryside

now, with fields all around me and only a few houses in sight. And I had no clue how to get back to A1A.

I hadn't been able to afford a built-in GPS when I'd bought my car, but Will had given me a Garmin for my birthday. I preferred it over my phone since it didn't eat up my limited data. It lived in my glove box for just such occasions, when I was in unfamiliar territory.

Driving one-handed, I leaned over and rummaged blindly until my fingers connected with the hard plastic case. I had it halfway out of the glove box when a meteor must have fallen from the sky and landed on the back end of my car.

I jolted forward, suspended from the seatbelt, my head now hanging down in the foot well of the passenger's side. My foot instinctively went to the brake.

Again, the car was slammed from behind. The back of my head cracked painfully against the underside of the dash, and everything went black.

,

CHAPTER SEVENTEEN

Someone was banging on my head and calling from afar, asking if I was okay.

No, I'm not okay, you ninny, since you're banging on my head.

I opened one eye and saw only gray fuzz. I blinked and my vision cleared somewhat. I was staring at carpeting.

The banging again. "Miss?" A male voice, muffled. "Are you okay?"

I put a hand on the gray carpet and pushed up. And saw stars when I banged my head again on the underside of the dash. I more carefully maneuvered myself into a basically upright position, muscles and tendons complaining loudly about how they had been twisted and yanked around.

My foot slipped off the brake pedal and the car lurched forward. I jammed on the brake again. Pain exploded inside my skull, but I managed to put the transmission in park.

"Miss?" A wavering voice from outside the car.

The air conditioner was blowing cool air against my face. My head cleared a bit. I turned it slowly toward my window and the concerned face of an elderly man hovering on the other side of the glass. Fumbling around, I found the button on the door. The window slid down.

"Miss, it's probably best that you don't move too much. I called 911. Paramedics are on the way."

I lifted a hand and felt around on my head. A tender lump on the back, but no stickiness, so hopefully no blood. I moved one arm up and down, flexed my hand, then the other arm and hand. I felt around my body. Some soreness on my belly and shoulder, where the seatbelt had dug into my flesh.

Releasing said seatbelt, I pushed open my door.

The elderly man, painfully thin in cutoffs and a baggy white tee-shirt, stepped back. He shook his gray head and clucked with concern. "You should wait for the paramedics."

"What happened?" It came out as a ragged whisper. I worked my dry mouth to get some saliva going.

"Looks like somebody rear-ended you, then took off. I heard the crash and got to my front window as fast as I could. A truck was pulling around you and speeding away."

"Lemme guess, a white pickup." I winced as I lifted one leg and then the other out of the car and set my feet on the ground. "You didn't happen to get the tag number, did you?"

"Afraid not. He was too far away by the time I got out here."

I tried to stand up. Nothing happened except a shot of pain down my back. The pain actually reassured me. It meant I probably wasn't paralyzed.

I grabbed the doorframe on each side and slowly pulled myself out of the car and to a stand. The process was not without agony, but everything seemed to be in working order, just stiff and sore.

I made it to the back of the car, with the elderly gentleman hobbling beside me, hands out. Ready to catch me I guess, should I start to go down. I'd probably crush him.

I was trying to figure out how to examine my banged-up bumper more closely without bending over—something that seemed beyond my capabilities at the moment—when a Florida Highway Patrol cruiser pulled up.

Ignoring the young trooper who climbed out of it, I continued to survey the injuries to my car. One fender was partially crumpled and the trunk lid was bent at an odd angle, but it was still closed. The damage could have been a lot worse.

I suspected the guy in the white pickup hadn't wanted to bang up his truck. He probably didn't have much worse than a few scratches on his front bumper.

Nonetheless I was very grateful that I'd decided to leave the dogs at Jake's. If my body felt like this after being bounced around, what injuries might they have suffered?

The lean, dark-haired trooper stopped three feet away, one hand on the belt buckle of his tan uniform. "What happened here?"

My good Samaritan started explaining and I let him.

When he'd wound down, I said, "Do you think it's driveable?"

A siren wailed in the distance, the approaching ambulance.

The trooper walked all the way around the car, stooped beside each of the back tires, leaned down even further to look under the carriage. He finally nodded. "I think so. Nothing protruding into the wheel wells or hangin' loose on the bottom."

The ambulance arrived and the two paramedics jumped out. One jogged over to us.

"I need to get back to town," It had occurred to me that this accident might be intended to delay me while somebody did something to the dogs. I struggled to rein in the panic that thought had triggered.

"Let the paramedics look you over first," the trooper said in a kind voice. "In the meantime, I need to see your license, for my report."

I had no intentions of letting the paramedics delay my departure. But I couldn't refuse to produce my license. I took a step toward the driver's door and pain jolted up my spine.

"I'll get it, ma'am," the trooper said.

I nodded. "It's in my purse, and could you get my phone too, in the console." I'd see if Larry could go check on the dogs, because I was beginning to think having the paramedics look me over would be a good idea.

The trooper returned with my purse. "I couldn't find your phone."

I opened my purse to retrieve my license and stared into it. It looked like confetti had been shoved into it. I realized belatedly that the pieces of paper and such were business cards, notes and receipts that had been stirred from the bottom. Also, the contents of my wallet had been dumped into the purse. Even my cosmetics bag had been violated, contents dumped out, and my compact had opened, sprinkling powder over credit cards and house keys.

I yanked the latter out and breathed a sigh of relief. The keys to Jake's house were still attached to the ring.

This guy was quick. He'd rifled my purse in the time it had taken the old man to get to his front window. Then I glanced at the elderly gentleman and adjusted my concept of how long that journey had taken.

I located my license in the bottom and handed it over. The trooper carried it to his cruiser.

I stumbled to the driver's side of my car and began searching for my phone. I finally found it under the car by the driver's door. How had it ended up there?

The old man had followed me. When I pointed to the phone, he picked it up and handed it to me.

Unfortunately, Larry didn't answer. I left a semi-hysterical message.

Then another horrible thought struck me. I checked my own voicemail.

The two saved messages from Mr. Gruff Voice were gone.

That explained the rifling of my purse and the mystery of how my phone transported itself to the outside of the car.

I'd ended up frustrating the paramedics after all. "You really ought to go to the hospital, ma'am," one of them insisted. "You could have a concussion."

I probably did and I was more than a little worried about why my back hurt so much. But nonetheless, I snatched my license back from the trooper when he held it out. I quickly thanked him and the old gentleman.

Then I climbed into the driver's seat of my car, my body strenuously objecting to the maneuver.

"We're going to need you to make a formal statement," the

trooper said. "These are serious charges, leaving the scene of an accident and–"

I waved a hand in the air. "I'll be talking to Sergeant Phelps of the Buckland County Sheriff's Department, as soon as I check on my dogs. All this is related to one of their cases." And with that, I took off, fumbling one-handed to turn on the GPS and find Jake's address under its history.

Quite a few ominous rattles emanated from the back end of my car. Best I could tell nothing fell off though. I wasn't sure my definition of *driveable* jived with the trooper's, but bottom line, I had to get to the dogs.

Jake's street was quiet mid-afternoon. I parked in his driveway, snatched up my purse and ran as fast as my battered body would allow to the front door.

Fumbling with the key, I finally got the door open. The alarm system beeped its warning that I had thirty seconds to turn it off, but I spent twenty of those seconds on my knees hugging two big dogs.

Then I called Sergeant Phelps. "You need to come here this time," I said as soon as he picked up.

"Why?"

"A Trooper Jacobs of the FHP just took a report on a hit-and-run traffic accident involving my car. I'm at Jake's." I disconnected.

By the time the good sergeant arrived fifteen minutes later, I'd downed two ibuprofen tablets and sixteen ounces of water, but I hadn't stopped shaking inside.

I gestured toward an armchair and settled my aching body onto the sofa. Then I gave him the whole rundown, including the bad news that the phone messages had been erased. "Doesn't this guy plowing into me on purpose prove that someone is determined to keep me from investigating? Which, in turn, means that Jake and Janey are innocent."

"You would think," he muttered under his breath. A little louder, he said, "I'll fill the sheriff in."

"Hey, did you find anything on that phone number, of the guy who threatened me?"

"Don't belong to anybody. Disposable cell most likely."

Crapola.

I also told the sergeant about the incident with the guard and my short run-in with Detective Wright. Phelps was scowling by the time I'd finished. "I don't know if Wright's really going to check into it," I added, "or if he was only saying that to get me to leave."

"I'll take care of it," he growled. "If it's the guard I think it is, we've had problems with him before."

"So, what's with Wright? He seems to have a chip on his shoulder."

He gave me a startled look, then his cop mask fell into place. "He's just busy. It's not every day we have a grand theft and murder investigation in this county."

"Is he looking into how all this might be linked to the other robberies along the coast?"

Another startled look. "How'd you hear about that?" I opened my mouth, but he answered his own question. "Sheriff Haines, of course."

Since he'd never met Will, I had to assume that the sergeant had checked me out. Not surprising. We'd checked him out.

"Look," I said, "is there something fishy going on in the sheriff's department here?"

He narrowed his eyes at me. "Who gave you that idea?"

"You did, that first time we talked, out on the sidewalk." Well, actually Becky had, but I wasn't going to get into all that. "It seemed like you were trying to tell me something, you know, between the lines."

"I was. I wanted you to check out the bikers, through Bach, 'cause I figured he could keep you safe. That's all."

"Oh, okay." I wasn't sure I totally believed him though.

He pushed up from the armchair. "But now it's gotten far too dangerous. You need to leave this alone."

With effort, I got myself upright to show him out. "I'm thinking that it's gotta be somebody fairly bright behind all these robberies." *Like a police detective*, I thought but didn't say.

Or that biker gang lieutenant, my subconscious mind offered up.

I told Phelps about going to the biker's bar—he paled some but didn't interrupt—and how that guy Loo had made a point of coming out to talk to Jojo and had later steered us toward Rusty Snyder.

"Okay, I'll check him and this Rusty out," the sergeant said, "but you need to quit now. Got it?"

"Don't worry. I'm done. I'm going to call Jake's lawyer right now and give him what I've got, then I'm packing my bags."

I said it with conviction. And I meant it... at the time.

CHAPTER EIGHTEEN

After the sergeant left, I locked up behind him and set the alarm. Then I dug around in my purse and found the list with Jake's lawyer's number on it.

As I spelled out what I had to the lawyer, I realized that nothing I'd found pointed to anyone else. It only cast doubt on Jake and Janey's guilt. So why was someone so bent on getting me to stop investigating?

"The strongest evidence of their innocence," I said, "is that someone is trying really hard to discourage me from checking this stuff out."

The lawyer, Caleb Gibbons, had hardly spoken up to this point. "Not likely I can use that in court," he said now, in a deep, pleasant baritone. "The prosecution would dismiss it as random coincidences, or maybe dig up some old enemy of yours who might be harassing you."

I started to say I didn't have any old enemies, but then I closed my mouth again. I did have some enemies, although they weren't very old ones. I'd helped Will put away some bad guys in the last few months.

The lawyer thanked me for all my help and then echoed Sergeant Phelps and my own common sense. "You should leave this alone now. I'll get my investigator on it."

After we'd disconnected, I remembered the Goldwing trike angle, which I'd neglected to put on my list. I should've called the lawyer back, but honestly I wasn't all that impressed with him or his investigator.

And I was now famished. It had been a long time since breakfast.

I foraged in the kitchen and got a veggie omelet going on the stove, then went looking for Janey's spices.

I found them in a narrow cabinet and pulled out a pepper mill and a jar of seasoned salt. My gaze fell on the phone book I'd left out on the counter.

After seasoning my eggs, I found myself leafing through the book as I waited for them to cook. Yes, there was a Honda dealership, on the outskirts of Daytona Beach, with a half-page ad, and right under it was another ad for Daytona Honda Motorcycles. It gave the same address so probably owned by the same people.

After all, I told myself as I slid the omelet onto a plate, my car might end up being totaled by the insurance company, if the bodywork's too pricey. I might end up needing a new car.

How would Mr. Gruff Voice even know that I went to Daytona Beach to look at Hondas?

Wait! Had he been following me? That thought gave me pause.

But people had jobs. Who had the time to follow me around all day?

Rusty, for one, my annoying inner voice said. And other members of the biker's gang, like that Loo guy. There probably weren't many of them who were gainfully employed, if Rusty's attitude toward making a living was typical.

I'd take some evasive actions, go around the block a few times to make sure no one was tailing me.

This time the dogs went with me.

This time something did fall off. I heard the clatter and clunk and saw pieces of metal in my rearview mirror, but traffic was heavy enough that I couldn't readily stop.

The car was still running so I forged ahead. After weaving in and out of some side streets, I was convinced no one was on my tail.

Half an hour later, I was showing my damaged car to a salesman on the used-car lot at Daytona Honda. He tsked and shook his head.

"I might be needing a new used car, or a used, new-to-me car rather."

He chuckled.

"But I can't afford to pay much." As in, not anything. I had no intentions of buying a car. The budget just wouldn't allow it, but if the insurance payout for the damage wasn't sufficient... I'd cross that bridge when I came to it.

He walked me over to a row of smaller Hondas. The dogs trailed along on loose leashes.

He eyeballed them, then steered me toward a 2013 silver CRV, a small SUV that was quite tempting.

"You don't rent cars, do you, or loan them out short-term?"

"You can take a test drive."

"No, I meant like let me drive it for a couple of days?"

He shook his head and opened his mouth, no doubt to sweeten the deal for the CRV.

"How about motorcycles?" I stood on tiptoe to stare across the lot at the shiny bikes lined up along one fence.

He looked a tad startled. "What about them?"

"Do you all ever loan them out?"

"I don't think so," he said. "You'd have to ask the salesman for the bikes. But you can't drive these two around on a motorcycle." He chuckled and gave me an indulgent smile.

I smiled back. "Only one of the dogs is mine." I pointed to Felix. "This guy's owner does take him out on his bike, in a sidecar."

"Wow, that's cool."

"I'm going to sleep on the idea of the CRV. In the meantime, I think I'll take a look at the bikes. Just for kicks."

"They're not cheap," the salesman warned as he gestured for me and the dogs to precede him across the lot.

Bless his heart, he trailed along and did the introductions to the motorcycle salesman. Once he'd wandered off, I went through the whole spiel again about my banged-up car and needing inexpensive transportation. While I was talking, I wandered over to the section of bikes that looked like Janey's, only with two wheels instead of three.

"Those are Goldwings. Top of the line. They're not cheap," he echoed the other salesman.

"Do you have any used ones?"

He looked at me, then the dogs, then back again. "A Goldwing's a lot of bike for a woman to handle, unless it's triked. You know what that is?"

I nodded.

"So happens I have one of those, used. Would you like to see it?"

I grinned. "Yes, please."

He led me to the other end of the string of bikes. And there was a shiny red trike, the twin of Janey's bike.

"How common are these?" I thought that was somewhat of an odd question but he didn't bat an eye. Maybe some bikers were into uniqueness.

"Red's one of our most popular colors in the Wing, and trikes are becoming more common. Folks often buy them, or get their own bikes triked, when they develop balance problems as they age. Would you like to take her for a spin?"

"Hmm, not today, because of the dogs. They can be a handful." I looked down at the two big dogs who had dropped to their bellies in the shade of the trike, tongues hanging out, panting quietly.

So make a liar out of me, you two.

"Has there been any other interest in it?" I congratulated myself on the great segue. That was certainly a question someone might ask, to see if they had to hurry to make a decision.

"A lady looked at it last week, but she hasn't been back."

Excitement bubbled in my chest. "Which day last week?"

He gave me a funny look. "Thursday, I think it was."

Yes! I mentally did a fist pump in the air.

"Did she test drive it?" The excitement crept into my voice, garnering me another funny look.

"Yeah."

"How long do people usually take the bikes out for, when they test drive them?" I knew *drive* probably wasn't the right lingo here, but I really didn't care if I was blowing my cover at this point.

"Usually ten or fifteen minutes."

"But she stayed out longer?"

"How'd you know that, and who the heck are you anyway? A cop or something?"

"Or something. Private investigator." I crossed my fingers behind my back and prayed he didn't ask for ID. "What did she look like?"

"Around your height and build, blonde hair, tanned skin, kind of leathery. I don't think she's a sunscreen enthusiast."

"How old would you say she was?"

He shrugged. "Probably about your age."

I nodded. "Don't let anyone buy or even touch that bike. The Buckland County Sheriff's Department will be in touch."

I signaled the dogs and headed back to my car as fast as my abused body would tolerate. With the dogs strapped into the backseat, I turned on the AC and then called Sergeant Phelps. I told him about the trike and the woman who'd test-driven it.

A beat of silence. "I guess I should thank you but you've gotta stop investigating. It's too dangerous now."

"Has the sheriff reopened the case?"

"Not exactly, but she'll probably agree to send somebody down to Daytona to check out that trike."

I wondered briefly how he was going to get around telling her where the tip came from. "Thanks, Sergeant. I'm really going to stop now. I'll be heading home tomorrow morning."

"Good. In the meantime, get back to Jake's, lock up tight,

and stay there."

"Yes, sir." I disconnected and gave the phone a mock salute. Then I grinned at the dogs in the rearview mirror. "Our work is done here."

A couple of minutes into the trip back to Buckland Beach, my phone rang. Becky's name came up on the dashboard screen. Not only was I delighted to hear from her, but talking on the phone would hopefully drown out the ominous rattles and clunks coming from my rear end.

"Hey, girl," I yelled at the Bluetooth speaker.

"Hey yourself," Becky yelled back. "We're home."

"Woohoo! I missed you."

"You too. How are you? How's Will?"

"We're fine. More important question, how was the trip?"

"Wonderful, romantic, expensive."

"And Andy?"

"He's fabulous," Becky gushed. "Sends his love."

"Back at him. Any man who makes you happy is my new best friend."

"Hey, I thought that was my title."

"Okay, second best friend."

A brief pause. "So how are you and Will, really?"

Dang, this woman knew me far too well.

"We're okay, although me being even further away, over here on the coast has been a bit of a strain."

"And…" she said.

"Why does there have to be an 'and?'"

"Because there always is with you and Will."

"Well, the issue of living together has come up a couple of times lately." I hesitated but decided that if you can't be honest with your best friend and all that. "And the kids issue once."

"And what did you say?"

"That I would consider the possibility of selling my house once the roof was fixed."

"Lordy, this man has the patience of Job."

"Hey, why are you taking his side?"

"Because I'm afraid he'll run out of patience eventually, and Will is the best thing that ever happened to you."

"I thought Todd was the best thing that happened to me at the time," I said.

A dramatic sigh came through the speaker. "Are the two men at all comparable?"

"No, my ex isn't even a man. He's a weasel."

"So what happened when the kids issue came up?"

"Will asked point blank why I was resistant to having them."

"And you said…"

"Nothing, because I don't know."

"Hmm, maybe you need to figure that out."

"I've been trying," I said. "All I know is that when Todd declared, after six months of marriage, that oh, by the way, he didn't want kids after all, I felt more relieved than disappointed."

"So?"

"So is that the reaction of a woman who'd make a good mother?"

Becky was silent so long, I thought we'd lost the connection. "Are you there?"

"Yeah," she said. "Something just occurred to me. Do you think maybe you were already sensing that your marriage was going to self-destruct, so you were relieved there would be no children to complicate things?"

"Maybe. I realized in therapy a few months ago that I'd known on some level for most of my marriage that I'd picked the wrong guy." Which was a huge part of my resistance to moving in with Will, and eventually marrying him. I didn't trust my own judgment.

"And knowing that, you were relieved Todd wasn't going to press you for kids."

My brain went into overdrive, then threatened to short out. "I'm gonna have to give that some thought."

"So, what's happening with this investigation of yours?" God bless Becky, she knows when to change the subject.

I filled her in, including about Mr. Gruff Voice. She was horrified and I quickly reassured her that I was done investigating and headed home in the morning. It felt so good to finally be telling people about the threats that I threw in Larry's attraction to me and his stolen kiss.

"Marcia, what are you doing?" Her voice went shrill. "Are you trying to sabotage your relationship with Will?"

I bristled. "No, of course not."

"Then why did you let him kiss you?"

"I didn't *let* him kiss me. He snuck up on me."

"Are you attracted to him?"

I gave that a moment's thought. "No, not really. More flattered that he's interested."

"And that's worth risking what you have with Will?"

"I'm not risking anything. I told Larry that I'm involved."

"Before or after he kissed you?"

"Before."

"Hmm, then he's not so good at respecting boundaries, now is he?"

"I guess not."

"He sounds like a player," Becky said.

I was real glad she couldn't see me as I felt my cheeks heat up. Why hadn't I seen that?

Because you were too busy being flattered, Ms. Snarky commented.

Crapola. For all I knew, the man was married.

"Look, I'm leaving tomorrow," I said. "I probably won't even see him again. So, tell me about the Bahamas."

Silence. Becky wasn't going to let me off the hook.

"Okay, I was stupid and naive, but I'm not used to men tripping all over themselves around me, like you are."

"Meow," she said, but with a chuckle in her voice.

I laughed as I entered the outskirts of Buckland Beach. "I'm almost back to the Blacks' house. How about I call you tomorrow after I'm home and we have a long catch-up session?"

"Sounds good," she said, and we signed off.

I breathed out a contented sigh. I was glad my bestie was home, even if she had held my feet to the fire.

My relief was short-lived. It was *deja vu* all over again on Jake's street, with sheriff's department cruisers and unmarked sedans, red and blue lights revolving on their roofs.

The front door was wide open and the two detectives and several deputies were once again tearing the living room apart.

"What are you doing?" I yelled gesturing with one hand, the dogs' leashes in the other.

Detective Wright gestured toward one of the deputies. "Call Animal Services."

"Unh-uh." I shook my head vehemently. "You're not taking these dogs anywhere."

"We're not allowed to leave them here," Lieutenant Harrison said in a gentle voice, "with no one to care for them."

My heart in my throat, I stared at him. "What do you mean?"

"I'm afraid you have to come with us. We have some questions for you."

My throat closed completely. Dumbfounded, I squeezed words out. "Are you arresting me?"

The lieutenant's eyes were soft, regretful. "Not yet. But you're under suspicion, for grand theft and an accessory in Elsie Belenky's murder."

CHAPTER NINETEEN

With effort, I collected myself, tried to focus on the issue of the dogs. "Let me call somebody to come take care of them."

"One call," the lieutenant said.

I took a deep breath. The irony did not escape me as I punched the name on my contacts. I was the one who was now calling a dog-sitter instead of a lawyer. Well, he was a lawyer, but not the kind I needed.

When Larry answered, I told him the situation.

He swore softly, then said, "How can I help?"

"Can you come take care of the dogs for this evening?"

"How about I bring them back to my place."

"Even better," I said, relief washing through me. That would put them beyond the reach of the law. I told him where to find the fake rock with the house keys.

"Do you have Jake's lawyer's name?" Larry asked. "I'll call him for you."

"Yeah. Caleb Givens. You know him?"

"Yes, he's good."

"Thank you so much, Larry."

"No problem. Try not to worry."

But I already was, more about how I would pay for the lawyer than about whether or not he could keep me out of jail. I didn't think that would be too hard, since they couldn't have any evidence against me.

My phone rang as soon as I disconnected. Caller ID said *Will*.

I started to answer.

The lieutenant wrapped his hand around mine, phone and all. "We've got to go. Sorry." He took the phone away from me.

He also took my purse strap from my shoulder.

He handed the dogs' leashes to one of the other men. "Make sure these guys don't get out."

With a hand firmly gripping my elbow, he led me out the door. At least he didn't handcuff me.

The humiliation of riding in the back of an unmarked police car—complete with a grill separating me from the backs of the detectives' heads and no inside door handles—was nothing compared to being left to cool my heels in a stark interview room. It contained only a metal table and three chairs, which seemed to be bolted to the floor.

The most disconcerting part was the one-way mirror lining one wall. Why did they even bother with the pretense of a mirror? Everybody who had a TV and had watched cop shows knew somebody was watching from the other side.

Did they watch you while you waited to be interviewed? Probably. I sat up straighter and tried to look cool, calm and collected, when my insides really felt like jello.

My heels were literally cooling. They'd taken my sneakers. Did they think I'd try to kill myself with the shoe strings?

The door finally opened and Lieutenant Harrison came in, followed by Detective Wright. Harrison announced their names and mine out loud, along with the date and time of day. Then he turned to me. "You're not under arrest at this time, Ms. Banks, but I'm going to read you your Miranda rights, just to be clear."

Just to cover himself legally was more likely. I was liking this guy less and less as time went by.

From a laminated card, he read the words that anyone who watches TV probably knows by heart. I was quite sure he knew them by heart as well. The card was for the benefit of the camera hanging from one corner of the ceiling. He finished with, "Do you understand these rights and do you waive your right for a lawyer?"

"Yes, and for now." I didn't want to look guilty by refusing to answer any questions, and I wanted to find out what they thought they had on me.

"Where were you this past Saturday," Harrison said, "between eleven-thirty a.m. and twelve-thirty p.m.?"

"At Jake and Janey Black's house until about twelve-twenty. I'm house-sitting and taking care of Jake's service dog." They already knew all this, since they'd asked these questions before. "Then I was driving to the pawn shop, to meet Larry Merrick, who was going to introduce me to the shop's owners."

"For what purpose?" Detective Wright asked.

"To talk to them about the robbery they'd had, to find out why they thought Jake and Janey had done it."

"In other words, to obstruct justice." Harrison's tone was sharp.

Yup, liking him less and less.

"No, that wasn't my intention."

"What was your intention?" the lieutenant asked.

"To help Jake and Janey."

Wright sneered. "By whacking Elsie Belenky on the head with a blunt object?"

"No! I found her already on the floor and bleeding."

"When did you find her?" Harrison asked.

"Around twelve-thirty. Then Larry, uh, Mr. Merrick came in, and I went outside to watch for the ambulance and police."

"How long would you say you were alone with Mrs. Belenky?"

"I don't know. No more than a few minutes."

I thought they were going to make me go through the whole business of what she'd said again, but Harrison changed tacks. "Have you been back to your house since staying over here on the coast at the Blacks?"

"Yes, once. I'm having some work done on my house. I went over to check on that."

"And perhaps to hide these?" He tossed a clear, sealed bag

on the table. In it was a soft, black cloth sack, about three inches high and two wide. Beside it were two clear stones, one large, maybe a quarter inch round, and one about half that size.

I swallowed hard. The uncut stones must be part of the haul from the robbery. "I've never seen those before."

"That's odd, because we found them buried in your backyard, and your footprint was in the dirt covering the hole."

I looked up at him, stunned. The soft spot in the yard that I'd blamed on moles.

I narrowed my eyes. "How'd you get a warrant to search my property?"

The lieutenant shrugged. "Wasn't hard, what with you being so cozy with the Blacks and sticking your nose in the investigation, and being the last person to see Elsie Belenky alive."

"Last of two people. Larry Merrick… she was still alive when he got there."

"Yes, but not for long," Wright said.

I tried to find a more comfortable position in the metal chair. My backache was getting worse. "You've known all those things for days. Why search my place and bring me in now?"

I expected them to refuse to answer, say something about how the cops ask the questions. But Wright grinned at me. "We got an anonymous tip that you were involved in the whole robbery ring."

"You are aware that I've received threatening calls to back off? And somebody even rammed the back of my car."

Wright looked a bit startled but covered it quickly. He opened his mouth.

The door opened and in stepped the sheriff herself.

Harrison indicated, for the sake of the recorder, that Sheriff Baker had joined the interview.

Then the petite woman paced back and forth on the other side of the table, repeating most of the questions that the detectives had already asked.

Feeling more than a little ganged up on, I gave her the same answers.

Suddenly she stopped pacing and planted both palms on the table, leaning partway across it. "Do you have any idea how much trouble you're in, Ms. Banks? We have enough evidence to arrest you as an accessory in multiple robberies."

She straightened and crossed her arms over her chest. "And murder. Although you may not be *only* an accessory there. After all, you were found hovering over her body."

I gritted my teeth and narrowed my eyes at her. And to think I'd been pleased, back when I was perusing those photos on the wall, that a woman had gotten herself elected sheriff.

"You all didn't treat me like a suspect then."

"We didn't know then what we know now."

"And what exactly do you know now?"

She smirked at me. "That you jumped out of your skin when Mr. Merrick found you there."

That gave me a moment's pause. Larry must have told them that more recently. Why had they interviewed him again? And why hadn't he told me about it?

The sheriff was waiting none too patiently for my response.

"I'd just found a woman on the floor," I said, "who'd obviously been robbed and then hit with something, and you find it surprising that I was startled when a man walked up behind me?"

"But you were supposed to meet him there?"

"Yes, but I'd never seen him before..." Well, except in his phone book cover photo. I opted to leave that out. "How was I to know he wasn't the person who'd just whacked Mrs. Belenky over the head?"

"That will be enough," an authoritative baritone voice said from behind me.

I swiveled around, which turned out to be a mistake. My back screamed at me.

A tall black man in a business suit stepped into the room. "I'm her lawyer."

Caleb Givens was a far better lawyer than I'd given him credit for. It had taken him less than an hour to poke a half-dozen serious holes in the case against me. He'd gotten the sheriff and the lieutenant to admit that the velvet bag was a common one used to carry gems, that the diamonds had no fingerprints on them, that there was no way to prove they were part of the diamond shipment stolen from the Belenkys' shop, that anyone could have buried them in my backyard, especially since I wasn't living there right now. And last but not least, that my footprint in the dirt on top of them only proved that I sometimes walked around in my own backyard.

Scowling at him, the sheriff finally said, "You may leave, Ms. Banks. Your purse and phone are out at the front desk."

I was debating between applause and kissing Mr. Givens's ebony cheek. I decided neither would go over well with either him or the representatives of law enforcement, so I reined in my inner imp.

I'd been in that interview room longer than I'd thought. It was dark outside. Mr. Givens insisted on walking me to my car. I thanked him again. "Um, how much do I owe you?"

He smiled for the first time, a delightful flash of white teeth across his face. "I think we'll make this entertaining evening *pro bono*, Ms. Banks. I've never been able to explode one of Lieutenant Harrison's cases quite so easily before."

I chuckled, but I had a funny feeling the good lieutenant knew he couldn't make much of anything stick against me. He was fishing. Unlike his partner, who seemed to truly have it in for me.

I thanked Mr. Givens one more time and climbed gingerly into my car. He pointed to the lock button on my door.

I dutifully locked myself in and then turned on my phone. There were four messages from Will—two voice and two text—increasingly frantic over the last few hours.

The last voicemail included background noises that sounded like a party. Will's voice yelled over the sounds of laughter and clinking glasses, "Marica, where the devil are you? Call me."

Dang, tonight was the dinner party the mayor of Collinsville was throwing for him. The party I'd begged off of, saying I had nothing appropriate to wear and wouldn't know how to act. In reality, I'd feared my presence would work against Will's reelection chances. There were many people in Collinsville for whom the sight of me would dredge up unpleasant memories.

I started my engine so I could turn on the AC, and called him back.

"Marcia. Thank God!" The sounds of cutlery scraping against dishes and murmured conversations in the background.

"Oh, Will. I'm sorry. Your party…" I was half a step away from sobbing.

"Never mind that." The background noises receded. "What's the matter?"

"They tried to set me up, as an accessory…" my voice hitched, "to murder!"

"They who?" his voice was gentle, soothing. A door closed in the background.

His efforts to calm me down had the opposite effect. I burst into tears. And then I was confessing everything—Mr. Gruff Voice's messages, the leather jacket guy in Cracker Barrel, the white truck trying to turn my car into an accordion, and the diamonds planted in my backyard. I ended with a promise that I was done with all of it and would be leaving in the morning for home.

"Why didn't you tell me all this sooner?" His voice was still gentle, which was more than I deserved.

"Um, I think mostly I didn't want to worry you."

"I would've come over and helped."

"I was afraid that you'd do just that. That you'd ditch your job to come here, which wouldn't be good with the election coming up."

"The election is nothing. Not compared to keeping you safe." I wasn't sure but I think he was a bit choked up.

I was more than a little surprised he wasn't bawling me out. "And I guess I thought you'd tell me again to leave it alone, that it was too dangerous."

A couple of beats of silence. I was about to ask if he was still there, when he said, "I realized something the other day, when I was doing those background checks for you. I chose this profession because I care about justice, and… Well, I finally got it that part of why I love you is that you care about justice too. So how can I fault you for pursuing it, even though you make me crazy with worry sometimes."

My chest swelled with warmth. "I'm sorry I make you crazy sometimes. But I do try to be careful. When I went to Rusty's with Jojo, I called Larry Merrick and he followed us, as my back-up."

"*I'd* much rather be your back-up in the future," Will said.

Something about that statement made my nether regions warm. "I'd prefer that too," I said in a sexy whisper.

"I'm coming over."

Reality smacked me upside the head. "No you're not. You need to get back to the party."

"It's winding down. They're serving dessert."

"Still, you're the guest of honor. You can't just leave." I glanced at my watch. "Will, it's almost nine. It would be close to midnight by the time you got here. There's an alarm system at the house. I'll be fine. Look, I'll call you when I get there and everything's battened down. Okay?"

A half-beat, then, "Okay. Love you."

"Love you too," I said, without hesitation for a change.

On the way to my temporary home, I called Larry. "Mr. Givens sprung me. He's really good."

"That's what I hear. You want me to bring the dogs over?"

"It's kinda late. Sure you don't mind?"

"Not at all. We'll be right there."

"Thanks."

Larry was as good as his word, arriving a few minutes after I got back to Jake and Janey's place. I'd barely had time to pop two more ibuprofen.

I dropped to my knees as the dogs ran through the door. They practically knocked me over. Felix's back end was wiggling so hard, I thought he'd dislocate something. Buddy licked my face.

Bubbles exploded in my chest. "Down, boy," I said with a chuckle.

He dropped to the floor, his black tail sweeping back and forth, his head tilted in that what's-up expression.

I laughed out loud.

"I'm jealous," Larry said, but he was grinning.

I started to stand up. It was a much slower and more painful process than normal.

Felix shifted his weight and braced his legs. I put a hand on his back and managed to stagger to my feet. I patted his head. "Thanks, boy."

Then I turned to Larry. "And thank you so much for taking care of them. You don't know what it meant to me to know they were safe."

Larry moved a couple of steps toward me. His grin now bordered on a smirk. "So now you owe me even more."

Say what? Boy, had Becky pegged this guy.

"Well, thank you again." I gestured vaguely toward the dogs. "It's getting late, so I think I need to bed these guys down."

"What?" His expression shifted to mock dismay. "After I went to all the trouble of writing this up." He held up a fistful of papers, then dropped them on the coffee table.

"What's that?" I said.

"The agreement for that training agency to sign," he sounded different, a little angry maybe, "giving you a year to produce a free dog."

Was he messing with me or was he really pissed about something? Butterflies danced in my stomach. "Great, thanks. Mattie said the agency will pay for having it drawn up."

"Yeah, but you still owe me." His face hard, he took another step toward me.

I moved back a half-step. "I don't think friends keep track of such things, do they?"

Suddenly Buddy was between us, blocking Larry's way. Felix stood up but made no move toward us.

Larry looked at the two big dogs, and then at me. His face shifted back to the expression he usually wore, one of amused observation. "Nah, of course not. I was glad to help." He smiled. "I'll call you tomorrow, okay?"

Without waiting for an answer, he turned and went out the open front door.

CHAPTER TWENTY

I ran to the door, slammed it shut and locked it. Then I raced to the alarm system and set it.

I dropped to my knees and hugged Buddy. "Good boy," I crooned in his ear. I wasn't real sure what had just happened with Larry, but the dog's intervention had seemed timely.

Or had I imagined that expression on Larry's face and the touch of anger in his voice? My counselor was always telling me to trust my instincts, but that didn't mean my perceptions were always accurate.

Still a bit shaken, I called Will back.

"Hey," he said without preamble, "I've been checking out auto body shops."

When did he have time to do that?

"There are a bunch of them in Ocala of course," he was saying, "but I'm not sure it's safe for you to drive your car that far. I found one in Ormond Beach that has a good reputation, lots of positive reviews online. Have you called your insurance company yet?"

"No. With all the craziness, I haven't gotten around to it." I hadn't even thought about it. "Where are you?"

Silence. No background noises.

"You're home," I said. "You blew off the rest of the party, didn't you?"

"I told them there was an emergency and I had to go."

"Will–"

"It was close enough to the truth, and I just couldn't stomach any more inane chitchat."

I shook my head and smiled at the phone. He was an excellent officer of the law, but good politician, not so much.

"Anyway," he said, "give the insurance company a call in the morning and see if they're okay with this shop." He gave me the name and address of the place. "I've got tomorrow afternoon off. I'll come over midday, and we can take your car there. Then I'll bring you home. How does that sound?"

"Sounds good. Thanks." I was suddenly wildly excited about going home. I was so done with Buckland Beach. "But fair warning. I'll be bringing two big dogs home with me. I'm keeping Felix until Jake and Janey get out of jail." Now that I'd seen their lawyer in action, I had much more confidence that they would indeed get out eventually.

"No problem."

I quickly called Mattie before it got any later. Now that I had the agreement in hand, I was anxious to find out what the board of directors had said.

She answered on the second ring with a crisp, "Hello." Phew, she hadn't been in bed yet.

I told her that my lawyer—I felt a little strange saying those words—had drawn up the agreement. "I hope it's okay," I said hesitantly, "he gave me a year to train a dog to replace Buddy."

"Marcia, that's fine. Take it easy. You're not going to lose Buddy."

I appreciated Mattie's attempts to reassure me, which was stepping a bit out of her comfort zone. She didn't normally acknowledge human emotions, except in a rather clinical way. Dogs, on the other hand...

Then again, the one human emotion she would be able to empathize with is the fear of losing one's four-legged best friend.

"Look," she said, "even if the board doesn't like this deal your lawyer's cooked up and they want to approach it a different way, you're not going to lose him. *We* made the mistake of not checking out the implications of the arrangement before we made it. But you have a contract saying Buddy is yours if you pay the monthly installments, which you've been doing. Our lawyer says that's binding. Buddy's yours. The only issue is how to keep it from screwing up our not-for-profit status."

It was the longest speech I'd ever heard her make. Air rushed out of my lungs in a big sigh. At least one problem was resolved. "Thank you, Mattie. I've been so afraid I'd lose him."

"Well, that's not going to happen." That crisp statement was more the Mattie I knew and loved. "A year is fine with me, but we'll pay back the money you've paid us for him right away. My guess is the sooner we do that, the better off we'll be legally."

Another surge of relief. I'd be able to pay for the repairs to my house after all.

We signed off.

Feeling much lighter and calmer than I had in days, I didn't even mind all that much that I was once again cleaning up the mess made by a police search.

In my suite, I didn't bother to put my jumbled belongings back in the closet or medicine cabinet. I jammed most of the stuff into my duffle bag, leaving out toiletries and fresh clothing for the morning.

The dogs watched me from the doorway, Buddy's ears perked, Felix's jowly face looking mournful.

Out in the living room, I put the sofa back together and re-shelved books. Then I picked up the sheath of papers Larry had dropped on the coffee table. Deciding I wasn't in the mood to read through them tonight, I took them into my bedroom and stuffed them in the top of my bag.

Then I went into Jake and Janey's bedroom. It wasn't in too much disarray, confirming my suspicion that this time the police were more interested in my things. Or maybe that's all they could get a warrant for, considering the Blacks had been in jail since the last search.

The dogs had followed me. Felix definitely seemed worried

that I was going to disappear again.

I leaned down and scratched behind his brindle ears. "It's okay, boy. You're coming too. See, we're taking your crate." I pointed to said crate, set up near Jake's side of the bed.

It was a large canvas-sided one. Yet another problem solved. It folded up for traveling. I unzipped the corners and collapsed it flat.

Buddy had stopped near the door and was sitting, watching me, but Felix was sniffing along the baseboard in the corner or the room.

I went looking for the carrying case that usually comes with such crates. When totally packed up, they look like an artist's portfolio. I found it folded and tucked behind Jake's nightstand. As I stood and shook it out, I heard scrabbling behind me in the corner.

I whirled around.

Felix was madly scratching at the edge of the carpeting. With dismay, I realized he'd torn a strip loose.

"No!" I signed for him to lie down.

He gazed at me, whined softly, but then complied.

I gingerly stooped down to examine the damage, and discovered that the edges of the strip were not torn. They had been cut, a clean straight cut with a razor blade or heavy-duty scissors.

Underneath, a small square had been cut in the floorboard. I dug a fingernail under one side and, with effort, pried the square of wood out.

In a hollowed-out hole under it rested a black velvet jeweler's bag.

I froze, my hand in midair, reluctant to touch it.

Since I doubted velvet held fingerprints very well, I finally convinced myself to pick it up. I dumped the contents out on the bed.

A gold ring—big black opal, with golden snakes entwined around it.

Heart pounding, I used the velvet bag like a dog poop sack and scooped the ring up without touching it. I turned the bag upright and jiggled the ring down inside, then pulled the drawstrings closed.

Not sure what else to do, I put it back where I'd found it.

Then I stood in the middle of the bedroom for several minutes, staring into space.

Had I been dead wrong about the Blacks? Were they thieves, and possibly murderers?

Wait, how did the police miss the ring? They'd searched the house so many times now, I'd lost track.

I looked down at the square of floorboard. Its cuts were not neat. Someone had sawed at the wood a bit to get that chunk out of there. I rolled the strip of carpet over it. The edges meshed and disappeared. Without knowing the carpet had been tampered with, one would never notice.

Still, why hadn't the police found it? Had someone planted the jewelry bag there recently? But who could've gotten in, past a deadbolt lock and an alarm system?

My mind flashed to the Army helmet key rack in the kitchen, and Janey's comment about all those lost keys floating around Buckland Beach. That would take care of the locks, but what about the alarm? Then again, I hadn't been setting it during the day when I went out, not until after the second call from Mr. Gruff Voice threatening the dogs.

Had someone from the sheriff's department planted the ring? Someone who was in on the robberies maybe, or taking bribes to ignore evidence that would clear the Blacks? My money was on Detective Wright.

But if that were the case, they would've pretended to find the bag and ring, not left it behind.

My tired brain was reeling. I decided to go to bed and try again to sort it all out in the morning.

But my sleep was fitful, punctuated by dreams of shadowy figures carrying little pouches of gems and jewelry, which they deposited in odd places, sometimes in the Blacks' house, sometimes in my own home.

Buddy woke me once. I must have been moaning or thrashing

around.

Finally, well after midnight, I drifted into a deeper sleep.

A cold nose against my elbow woke me. Dim light filtered through the bedroom curtains. Buddy's chin rested on the side of my bed, his eyes worried.

"Wha's the matter, boy?" I muttered. Had I overslept? I didn't think I'd been dreaming again. "You need to go out?"

Sounds of movement in the living room jolted me upright and out of bed.

CHAPTER TWENTY-ONE

I grabbed my robe and raced to the door of my suite.

Leaning over, I put my ear to the wooden surface. Multiple voices—several male, one female— and a low woof from Felix.

I shrugged into my robe and eased the door open a crack to peer out.

Janey and Jake stood in the middle of the room. A deputy was crouched down, attaching something to Jake's ankle. Felix leaned gently against the other leg, Jake's hand resting on his head.

The deputy grimaced and shuffled away from Felix's doggy breath.

I smiled and opened my door wide.

Another deputy was fooling with a big black box on a shelf near the door, and Sergeant Phelps stood at parade rest by the door itself.

"Good morning, everyone," I said cheerfully.

Jake and Janey smiled at me. "Good morning, Marcia," Janey practically sang out. "We're home."

The sergeant raised an eyebrow in my direction, then dipped his head slightly. "Ms. Banks."

"And we have these lovely anklets." Janey lifted her foot in the air. "Compliments of the sheriff's department." She grinned at Sergeant Phelps.

He pretended to ignore her but his eyes twinkled.

I wondered if he'd played some part in getting the Blacks released with house arrest, perhaps using the incident with the guard as leverage.

"All done, Sarge," the deputy by the black box said. "Folks, you've got a nine-hundred-foot radius from the box. You should be able to go out to the street to check your mail, sit on your lanai and go anywhere in the house. Beyond that and you'll set off an alarm."

"I can't go out to my shop?" Jake said.

Janey put a hand gently on his arm. "There's not much to work on right now anyway," she said in a low voice.

He grimaced and nodded. "Thank you, Deputies, Sergeant." He headed for the door, I presumed to show them out, but then he swayed and staggered a step sideways.

Unfortunately, it was away from Felix, but the bulldog was quick for all his bulk. He was around his master and bracing his legs in less than a second. The jumble of arms and legs and doggy limbs was confusing, but when they'd sorted themselves out, Jake had managed to keep himself from falling, with a little help from his dog.

"I'll get his vest," I murmured. I'd left it with Buddy's in my room.

When I came back with it, the deputies were gone. Jake sat on the sofa, his head in his hands. I could hear Janey puttering in the kitchen.

"We've got six eggs," she called out. "How does scrambled with cheese sound?"

Jake didn't respond.

"Sounds wonderful," I called back, as I set the vest down beside Felix, who was lying on the floor, his many chins resting on one of Jake's shoes.

I moved to the kitchen doorway. "I used some of the eggs and veggies. I'll do a Publix run for you all before I leave."

"That would be great." Janey lifted her head from her work at the stove to give me yet another big smile. "Breakfast in ten minutes."

At least one of them seemed no worse for wear after a week

in jail.

I turned back toward the guest suite.

Jake lifted his head and looked at me as I walked by. His eyes were haunted, his skin tinged with gray under his tan. He'd aged ten years in the last few days. "Thank you for everything, Marcia. We couldn't have survived all this without your help."

I stopped moving, wanted to protest, but I decided just to accept graciously. "You're welcome." Then I darted into my room to get dressed before breakfast.

The morning went by quickly. Jake seemed to recuperate some from the ordeal of being in jail, as it slowly sank in that they were home now. His color was closer to normal by the time I'd finished my packing and went in search of Janey to get her grocery list.

I was rattling down the road toward Publix when I remembered the ring in the velvet bag. What the heck should I do about it?

I was tempted to call Will and ask his opinion, but I was pretty sure he'd tell me to call the sheriff's department and report having found it.

Part of me knew that's what I should do, but most of me couldn't bear the thought of them hauling Jake and Janey back to jail. I had no idea what the provisions of their bail might be. Would more evidence cancel out the arrangement?

I wished I could forget that I'd ever seen the dang thing.

I tabled the decision about what to do while I gathered the groceries on Janey's list and paid for them with the credit card she'd given me.

Halfway back to their house, my phone rang. It was Larry.

I was still annoyed by his you-owe-me comments and was sorely tempted to ignore the call, let it go to voicemail. But I didn't. Maybe he was calling to apologize.

"Marcia." His voice was loud. Background noises said he was standing outside and near a road. "How are you doing this morning? Has your body recuperated from your fender bender?"

I wanted to tell him that my body was none of his business, and that someone intentionally ramming into you was a bit more than a fender bender.

But I managed to hold my tongue. "I'm fine."

"Hey, I know you said you were done investigating, and I don't blame you, but this may be a golden opportunity to search Rusty's place more thoroughly. I saw him and his girlfriend go into a bar on A1A."

Apparently, he was going to pretend nothing had happened last night, which had me questioning my perceptions all over again.

"I'll go in there," Larry was saying, "and keep them occupied, buy a few rounds of beers if need be. And you can go over to his place and look around. Text me when you're done. If they leave here before you do, I'll call you so you can get out of there quick. Sound like a plan?"

No, it sounded like something I shouldn't do.

But then I turned into Jake's driveway and pulled all the way back, so it would be easier to carry the groceries in through the kitchen door.

Jake and Janey were sitting on their lanai in matching lounge chairs, cold glasses of iced tea on the small table between them. Janey saw me, smiled and waved. She pushed herself to a stand and headed my way.

"I don't know where he lives," I said, stalling. "Jojo took me last time."

"Okay, I'll get Jojo to pick you up. He can help you search."

"Larry, wait…" But he was gone.

Janey was now standing beside my car, so I got out. She and I carried the groceries inside and put them away. Then she rejoined Jake and Felix on the lanai.

I stood inside the sliding glass doors and watched as Jake reached over and took Janey's hand.

And several decisions were suddenly made. I was a third wheel here. It was time to leave. But I had an hour to kill before

Will would arrive.

The Blacks were out of jail but still a long way from being cleared of the charges against them. And whoever was framing them had now tried to implicate me as well. Would they plant more evidence against me?

Maybe I should go check out Rusty's place more thoroughly, since Larry was keeping them occupied. And Jojo would be with me.

I went into my room and grabbed my duffle bag and the plastic bag with Buddy's supplies. "Come on, boy."

We went out back through the slider so I could say goodbye to Jake and Janey. They thanked me several more times, and I said goodbye to Felix with a good ear scratch.

I parked partway down the block, near the corner. Leaving the car and AC running, I got out and leaned against my front fender.

I was seriously considering canning this whole idea and killing time with an iced coffee at Dunkin' Donuts instead, when Jojo careened around the corner and flew toward me. I flagged him down.

He slowed as he went past me, then made a U-turn and eased to a stop beside me.

"I'm not sure about this, Jojo."

"Me neither, but I figure if ole Rusty slips past Bach, we can just pretend we came back to take a second look at the bike he's sellin'."

It was a plausible excuse.

Feeling somewhat more confident, I nodded. "I've got to meet a friend right after this, so I'll follow you."

"Aw shucks." Jojo grinned at me. "I thought I was gonna have the pleasure of having a pretty lady ride on my bike with me again."

His grin was hard to resist, and I found his disheveled state more tolerable now that I knew he was a harmless retiree instead of a ruthless outlaw biker. I smiled back. "Maybe another time."

When pigs fly, Ms. Snarky said inside. For once, I agreed

with her.

When we were out on A1A, I called Will. It went straight to his voicemail. I left a message that I'd meet him at the auto body shop.

Rusty's place was in the general direction of Ormond Beach.

I disconnected and then decided to make another call, to be on the safe side.

"Sergeant Phelps."

"Hi, Sergeant. This is Marcia Banks." I told him I was headed with Jojo to check out Rusty's place.

"That's not a good idea," he said.

"It should be safe. Larry Merrick is keeping him and his girl-friend occupied at a bar. He's going to call me if they leave. And we won't break into anything. We're only going to poke around outside."

"Bach? He's keeping them occupied?" He sounded a little surprised.

"Yeah. He said he likes Jake and doesn't want to see him get screwed. And you're the one who connected me up with him, remember?"

"Because he knew most of the bikers around here. And because he's got an eye for a pretty lady so I knew he'd look out for you. Keep you out of trouble." A pause, then in a gruffer voice, he said, "That hasn't worked out so well."

I resisted the urge to defend myself, especially since this was the man who'd suggested I investigate to begin with.

"I guess they've truly buried the hatchet then," Phelps said.

"What do you mean?"

"Jake took Janey away from Bach, back in high school."

"What? I thought Jake and Janey met after he got out of the Army, the first time that is."

"No, that's when they got back together. Janey was Bach's girl—rumor was they were gonna get married. And then Jake asked her to his senior prom, and she dropped Bach like a hot potato."

"How do you know all this?"

"Bach, Janey and I were in the same class, at Buckland High. Jake was a year ahead of us."

I adjusted my assumptions about the sergeant's age. He must be graying prematurely.

"Hmm, interesting," I said. "Hey, we're almost there." Jojo had put his left blinker on. "I just wanted someone to know where we were, in case something goes wrong."

"It's about time for my lunch break. I think I'll mosey over that way and hang out nearby. Give me a shout if you need me."

Muscles relaxing throughout my body told me I'd been more uptight about this whole deal than I'd thought. "Thank you, Sergeant."

"No problem." He disconnected.

I followed Jojo onto the unpaved road where Rusty lived. He pulled his bike into the driveway, which was nothing more than two strips of packed gravel across a scraggly lawn. I opted to park on the side of the road.

Before getting out of the car, I put the sergeant's number on speed dial. Then I let Buddy out of the backseat and attached his leash to his collar, leaving his service vest in the car.

We trotted down one of the gravel tracks to the metal building that was Rusty's garage and shop, and apparently his main storage area for junk. Like before, the double metal doors were hanging open.

Jojo peeled away from me. "I'm gonna check the house," he called back over his shoulder.

"Wait."

No response.

"Jojo," I yelled.

Either he was ignoring me or his hearing wasn't the greatest because he kept going.

So much for my promise to the sergeant that we'd just poke around outside.

Starting at one end of the garage, Buddy and I worked our

way methodically inward. I had him on a loose leash, hoping maybe he'd sniff out some evidence hidden amongst the motor-cycle parts, tools and other random objects.

The fans were off and the building was stifling hot. Sweat rolled down the sides of my face and along my spine. I consid-ered turning the fans on but was afraid the noise would keep me from hearing anyone approaching. I quickly pulled my hair up into a ponytail.

I kept nervously checking my watch as we investigated the rows of junk. Buddy trailed behind, also checking out tantalizing smells, and sneezing occasionally from the dust. Whenever he'd stop and sniff a particular box for any length of time, I'd double-back and give it a more careful examination. But all we'd uncov-ered so far were more metal objects, many slimy with grease.

I jumped when Jojo's shadow darkened the doorway. "House is locked up tight," he informed me.

Recovering myself, I said, "How long do you think Larry, I mean Bach, will be able to keep them occupied?"

"Pretty long, if he's buyin' 'em beer."

My queasy stomach settled down some, and I went back to my search. Of course, it would help if I knew what I was searching for.

Jojo started on the other side of the garage.

Buddy and I were almost to the middle of the back of the building when I came across those black metal strips again. Remembering Rusty's warning about their sharp edges, I moved them carefully and found a wooden crate underneath them. In the crate was more of the black metal, one piece bent into a three-sided box of sorts, another into a long curved strip, the ends trimmed to round them off.

"Hey, Jojo, come here."

He came over and stood beside me, staring into the crate.

"What do you think they are?" I asked.

When he looked up at me, his skin had gone a bit pale under his tan. "I'd say they were parts of a fake fender, to make a regu-lar ole Harley look like an Indian bike."

Excitement bubbled in my chest as the implications sank in. We'd found the evidence that would clear Jake and Janey.

A muffled thump on the other side of the metal wall made us both jump. Jojo took off out of the building and around the side to investigate. Buddy and I followed.

But there was no one around the back of the building but Jojo.

I slowed as a flash of white some twenty feet away caught my eye. The front of a white truck backed in under the live oaks. Buddy and I went over to investigate. Sure enough, it was a pickup, and its front bumper was dented and scratched, rather badly.

"Hey Markie, come here," Jojo called out.

We jogged back over to where he stood near the fridge full of beer.

He was frowning at the sagging door of a dilapidated shed that had been tacked onto the back of the building. "I thought I heard somethin'."

I turned my head and pushed a loose clump of hair behind my ear, leaning forward a little. A faint shuffling noise. It sounded like it was coming from the shed.

"Could be mice," I said. *Or rats!* I suppressed a shudder.

Another faint sound, maybe a moan.

"Mice don't make that kinda noise," Jojo said.

Buddy was sniffing around the crack under the door. He scratched at the ground in front of it and whined softly.

"He smells somethin'," Jojo pointed out the obvious.

A louder thump and the door shook. Buddy turned and looked at me, tilted his head to one side.

"Come here, boy." I wanted him out of the way because Jojo had grabbed the small crowbar that was jammed into the latch on the door, essentially locking it so anyone inside couldn't get out.

Buddy and I stepped farther away as Jojo struggled with the bar. It suddenly came loose and he staggered backward a few steps.

The door swung open and a man fell out, face first in the dirt.

"Well, I'll be…," Jojo said, dropping the bar to the ground.

I squinted to see inside the shed. Sitting on the floor was a medium-sized, thirtyish blonde with leathery skin. Rusty's girl-friend, I presumed. And no doubt the woman who'd test-driven the red trike at the Honda dealership for an exceptionally long time.

We'd found the robbers alright, but there were two points of confusion. One, they were supposed to be in a bar on A1A.

Two, they were tied up with thick ropes, duct tape over their mouths.

CHAPTER TWENTY-TWO

Jojo pulled out a pen knife, then stared at it. "This ain't gonna cut it."

"Literally," snarky me said before I could muzzle her.

"We need to find somethin' to cut 'em loose with."

I shook my head. "I vote for leaving them tied up and calling the police."

Ignoring me, Jojo jogged back toward the doorway of the metal building, presumably to find said sharp object inside.

I managed to roll Rusty over and then grabbed one end of the duct tape on his mouth.

He let out a howl when I ripped it off, then swore profusely. I couldn't blame him. A fair amount of brick-red beard and mustache had come off with the tape.

"Who tied you up?" I asked.

That set off a fresh round of cursing. This one seemed to be aimed at someone who'd double-crossed him. But he only half made sense and he wasn't naming names.

I shook my head again and got out my cell phone, hit a speed dial number. The phone rang once.

Buddy's leash whipped around my legs as he dashed behind me. I struggled to keep my balance. "Hey," I said into the phone, "we–"

Buddy growled as a hand wrapped around mine, yanking the phone from my grasp.

"Wha'?" Heart pounding, I whirled around.

Larry Merrick stepped back, my phone in one hand, a pistol in the other. He hit the button to disconnect my call, then said, "Control your dog."

"Sit," I squeezed out of a tight throat.

Buddy's rump hit the ground, but his eyes stayed on the intruder.

I wasn't particularly surprised to see Larry. Since Rusty and his "old lady" weren't where they were supposed to be, it followed that he wouldn't be either. On some level, I'd guessed he was involved, after last night, but didn't want it to be true.

The planted ring... and I'd so helpfully steered him to the keys in the fake rock. Or had he swiped a set from the Army helmet key rack during that party he'd mentioned, or perhaps picked up one of Jake's lost sets at a bikers' club meeting months ago?

I stared at him. "Elsie wasn't saying 'No, Jake Black,' was she? She was saying 'No, take back,' or maybe 'Not Jake, Bach.'"

He smiled. "Finally figured that out, did you? And you so obliging went out to flag down the ambulance too."

My chest tightened. I felt nauseous. "You hit her again." I could hardly get the words out.

Then I realized I needed to keep him talking. "But why'd you take me to Jojo's and talk to all those other bikers to get them to help?"

"Window dressing, to throw you off. I never dreamed old Jojo would come up with a lead. And the bumbling idiot actually stumbled on a good one at that. Shame he led you to Rusty, 'cause then I had to work harder to discourage you."

Said bumbling idiot came around the corner of the building, fifteen feet away, an old machete in his hand.

I shook my head ever so slightly.

Jojo froze, his eyes wide. Then he slowly started backing up.

Oh, Larry, you so underestimate Jojo.

Barely in time, he disappeared back around the corner.

Larry stepped farther away from me and shifted his position, angling himself so that he could watch me and Rusty, but also both corners of the building and the door into the garage.

It dawned on me that he was waiting for Jojo to show up. Fear that the old man would try to be a hero made my chest hurt. I had to distract Larry.

"You planted those diamonds in my yard, and that ring in Jake's house, didn't you?"

"Oh, you found it." He glanced my way. "What'd you do with it?"

"Threw it away."

He grinned. "I don't believe you."

Not surprising. Did I mention I'm a lousy liar?

He'd gone back to watching the corners of the building, his eyes flicking back and forth. "I'll be calling the sheriff's department with another anonymous tip, once I wrap things up here."

"And the white pickup." I gestured toward the truck under the trees, but this time he didn't shift his gaze. "Is that yours? You sure do have a lot of vehicles."

"No, it belongs to Rusty. He hit your car a little harder than I'd intended."

I flashed to a pants leg as someone got into a white pickup, the day I'd arrived at Jake's. "And Rusty switched out the Indian's saddlebags, didn't he?"

"That was me. I borrowed his truck. Couldn't trust him to do that." He glanced at Rusty, still trussed up at my feet. "He's not the brightest bulb in the package."

Rusty had been quiet up to this point, but now he let out another string of expletives.

Larry sneered at him. "Shut up, you idiot. If you hadn't said my name in front of Elsie…"

Another piece fell into place. He also hadn't trusted Rusty to pull off the diamond heist on his own, so he'd shown up. Bile rose in my throat. No wonder Larry had been so willing to drop everything that day and introduce me to the pawn shop owners. He'd used his meeting with me as his excuse for being there.

But then Rusty had said something that gave away his

connection to the robberies.

Larry was shaking his head. "Should've known better than to try my set-up so close to home, but that gold jewelry was too tempting. And then Phil told me about the diamonds."

"Phil?" My voice went up in surprise. "Phil Sanford, the laundromat guy?"

"Yeah. He kept an eye on the Belenkys for me, let me know when something good had come in."

I shook my head. Sanford wasn't the "simple soul" I'd assumed he was. Instead, he was a darn good actor.

"I'd planned a couple more hits," Larry said, "but Buckland Beach's finest were sharper than I thought they'd be. They figured out that it was Jake and Janey too soon."

"Except it wasn't them. You set them up." That came out sharper than was probably wise.

"Enough, Marcia." Larry's face hardened. "I'm not gonna stand here all day satisfying your curiosity." He swung his head back and forth in mock sadness. "I gave you so many warnings, so many opportunities to back away from all this. But no, you couldn't leave it alone."

He wiggled his gun slightly. "Where's Jojo?"

"I don't know. He went up to the house earlier."

Apparently this was close enough to the truth that I pulled it off. Larry nodded.

"Move away from Rusty."

I stepped aside a couple of paces, moving Buddy back with me.

He glanced again at both corners of the building, then back at me. "Now, how am I going to work this? Marcia, what you do for me in the next few minutes will determine if I leave you dead, along with these two, or take you with me."

"With you where?"

"I've got quite a bit of money stashed in a bank in the Caymans, but we don't have to live there. We can go anywhere you like in the Caribbean, or South America."

I was thinking of where I'd like him to go, preferably with my shoe planted in his keister to send him on his way. But I reined in my temper. "Buddy goes too."

"Sure, we can take the mutt." But something flickered in his eyes and I knew he was lying.

But then so was I. I had no intention of going anywhere with him. "What do you want me to do?"

"Untie the woman, then she can untie Rusty. It needs to look like they shot each other. A falling out amongst thieves, or perhaps a lovers' quarrel. Which way do you think we should stage it, Marcia?" He exaggerated the three syllables of my name, confirming my suspicions.

He was just toying with me, enjoying the power.

I dropped Buddy's leash—if need be, I'd signal him to run, but not unless I had to. Larry might try to shoot him.

I gestured toward Buddy, but not the stay signal. Instead, I held my hand up in the air, palm out, my wait-for-more-guidance signal. His body tensed, his version of standing at attention.

Then I stepped into the shed. "This is gonna hurt." I pinched a corner of the duct tape and yanked it off the woman's mouth.

"Yow!" She glared at Larry and let out a string of expletives that made Rusty's seem tame.

Meanwhile, I struggled with the knot of the rope wrapped around her arms and torso. It began to loosen.

"Why are you helping him?" the woman snarled under her breath. "He ain't gonna take you with him. He's gonna kill you and the mutt."

"I know," I whispered, as I slowly unlooped the rope, stalling for time. I started on the knot at her ankles.

I figured Larry might take me with him initially, as his insurance policy. But eventually I'd become a liability. I glanced out the door of the shed to where Buddy stood watching me. My chest tightened. My dog would become a liability much sooner.

That is, *if* Larry really intended to leave the country. He was going to a lot of trouble to cover his tracks.

Scrabbling sounds from above, then an elephant stampeded across the metal roof.

Larry jerked his head up.

I ran out of the shed, planning to keep running while he was distracted. I opened my mouth to yell for Buddy to follow me.

But the sight of Jojo flying over the edge of the roof stopped me in my tracks, my mouth still hanging open.

He landed on Larry, knocking him to the ground. They rolled over and over, hugging each other in a wrestlers' clinch.

I raced over, my eyes darting around, frantically looking for the pistol.

Unfortunately, it was still in Larry's hand. The hand came up and he brought the gun butt down on Jojo's head.

CHAPTER TWENTY-THREE

Larry Merrick scrambled out from under Jojo's limp body. "I wondered where you were, old man." He pointed the pistol at Jojo's head and growled, "Payback for getting in the way."

"That's hardly fair," I yelled. "You dragged him into it."

He glanced at me, then Jojo moaned. Larry's eyes and aim jerked back to him. "This is better still. Jojo and Rusty fought it out, and Rusty's old lady got in the way."

"I don't think so," a hard voice from behind us. "Don't move, Bach."

I whirled around. Sergeant Phelps was standing at the corner of the building, his pistol in both hands out in front of him.

About time!

Merrick made a grab for me, no doubt to use me as a shield, but Buddy was between us in a flash.

Merrick fell over his broad back and I stomped on his gun hand.

More howling and swearing. I'd have to wash my ears out after this.

Buddy skittered backward, out from under Merrick, and the man landed with a thump on the ground.

Phelps was beside me, snatching up the gun, pocketing it and then grabbing for Merrick's arm to haul him to his feet. I stepped back.

Rusty's "old lady" had gotten her feet loose. She struggled to a stand and took off running, hands still tied behind her.

Phelps snorted. "She won't get far. Back-up's on the way."

"What took you so long?" I said, sounding more churlish than I'd intended.

He glanced at me. His lips were pinched into a tight line, but his eyes twinkled. "You were doing such a good job of getting him to confess. I didn't want to interrupt."

Jojo moaned. I ran over to him and helped him to sit up on the ground.

"You okay, Jojo?" the sergeant called over from where he was handcuffing Merrick's wrists together.

"Yeah, I think so." He rubbed his head and winced. I gingerly parted his matted hair. A lump was beginning to form but I didn't see any blood.

"You weren't supposed to try to fly, old man," Phelps said, but with affection in his voice. "You were just supposed to distract him."

Tires crunched on gravel on the other side of the building. Multiple tires from the sound of it.

"Back here," Phelps yelled. "I've got them secured."

The first person around the corner was the diminutive sheriff, her weapon drawn. She screeched to a halt, quickly surveyed the situation and holstered her pistol. Loping over to the sergeant, she said, "What've we got?"

The second person around the corner, a deputy, was dispatched by the sergeant to chase down Rusty's girlfriend. "She won't be hard to recognize," Phelps called after him with a chuckle in his voice. "She's the one with her hands tied together."

The third person to come around the corner was Will. I ran to him, Buddy racing along beside me.

Will grabbed me and held me tight. "You okay?"

"Yeah, we're fine." Not the complete truth yet. I was still shaking some from excess adrenaline. I leaned back in his arms to look up at him. "But how'd you know I was here?"

"I was on A1A and the sheriff's cruiser went flying by, no siren but lights flashing. I had a gut feeling it had something to do with you, so I followed her."

I wasn't sure how to take that. I opted to change the subject. "You didn't get to save the day this time." I smiled up at him. "Sergeant Phelps did."

Will stared down at me and slowly shook his head. Then he kissed me soundly.

When we came up for air, Sheriff Baker was standing nearby. "I owe you an apology, Ms. Banks. I don't like to encourage civilian interference, but in this case, I'm glad you were stubborn enough to keep investigating."

"Only my mother gets to call me stubborn, Sheriff," my snarky self said.

"And me," Will said, grinning down at me.

Suddenly the sheriff's face lit up with a big smile. "*Determined* then. Thank you for your assistance."

"You're welcome." I let go of Will long enough to shake the sheriff's hand.

Two hours later, Will and I were sitting in Sergeant Phelps's office while someone typed up my statement.

"Are you sure you're okay?" Will asked for the hundredth time.

"Yes, I'm fine." Other than feeling like an idiot for trusting Larry Merrick. No wonder Mr. Gruff Voice always knew what I was up to.

"I'm worried about Buddy though." I leaned over and ran my hands along his back yet again. "Merrick fell pretty hard on him."

Will leaned over too, watching Buddy's face. "He's not reacting to your touch. I think he's fine."

I snickered and, still hovering over Buddy, turned my head to smile at Will. "We're gonna be a pair of those helicopter parents you read about, aren't we?"

He stared at me.

I gulped a little when I realized what I'd said. Then I let out a shaky laugh. "I guess I'm starting to get used to the idea."

The door opened at that moment, praise the Lord, and Sergeant Phelps came in, holding several sheets of paper. He placed them in front of me. "You wanna read those over and then sign them, Ms. Banks."

"Sure." I picked up the first page. "But you'd think after all we've been through together, you could call me Marcia."

Phelps rolled his eyes. "Honestly, Ms. Banks, and please don't take this the wrong way, but I'm hoping we never have occasion to get to know each other any better."

Will let out a bark of laughter.

I ignored him as I skimmed the statement. Then I signed it and handed it back to Phelps with a smile. "Does this mean you don't want me to stop by to say hey when I come back to pick up my car?"

The sergeant snorted softly. "Uh, speakin' of which, you know that deputy I assigned to drive it back for you. He had to get it towed in. The muffler fell off in the first block and was dragging on the road."

For some reason that struck me as funny. Will and I looked at each other and we both burst out laughing.

The corners of Phelps's mouth quirked up. "Lemme know the address of the shop you were gonna take it to and I'll get it towed there, courtesy of the Buckland County Sheriff's Department."

"Thanks," I said. "Have you heard anything from the hospital about Jojo?"

"Treated and released." Phelps flashed a brief grin. "His head's pretty hard."

"Tell him thanks for me, for helping you save us." I knew I should go by and check on him, but suddenly I was exhausted. I'd give him a call tomorrow to see how he was doing.

"Thanks, Sergeant." Will stood and gave him a hearty handshake. "Come on, Marcia, we gotta get moving." He looked at his watch and grimaced.

The sergeant extended his hand to me. "Take care of yourself, Ms. Banks."

"I will." I reached out, but then the imp in me took over. I grabbed his hand and pulled him into an awkward hug. "Thanks for everything."

His tanned cheeks were a bit ruddy as we left his office.

CHAPTER TWENTY-FOUR

I must have fallen asleep on the way back to my place.

My last coherent memory was of conveying my worries to Will about what kind of mess I would encounter, between the construction and the police search. I was imagining the kind of chaos they'd left behind at Jake and Janey's.

"Stop worrying," Will had said. "Edna and Mrs. Wells said they'd clean the place up."

I vaguely wondered how they would get in…

"Marcia, wake up," Will said. "We're home."

Never had two words—well, three if you broke down the contraction—sounded so marvelous.

We were home!

I opened my eyes, tilted my head to the left, and smiled at my handsome chauffeur.

He got out and released Buddy from his safety strap in the backseat.

I was kind of missing Felix, but it was a very good thing that he was home with Jake, where he belonged.

Will came around to my side of the car. With a grin, he bowed and then gestured toward my front door. "Milady?"

A twinge of guilt as I flashed to climbing into Larry Merrick's SUV. I shook it off along with all thoughts of Merrick…the weasel.

I took Will's proffered hand and faked a deep South accent. "Why thank you, kind sir."

We walked up the sidewalk hand in hand, Buddy beside me.

Will stepped forward. "You got your key handy?" he asked over his shoulder, louder than necessary on such a quiet afternoon.

Ah the quiet, the blessed quiet! No hammering sounds, not even from the direction of the new motel.

"I seem to have misplaced mine," Will added.

I dug out my keys and he unlocked the door, then stepped back to let me go first.

As I crossed the threshold into the dim house, lights flared on and people jumped out of everywhere, yelling, "Surprise!"

I froze, my jaw dropping. The place was spotless.

Edna Mayfair, in her favorite bright red muumuu, danced in little circles under a *Welcome Home* banner strung above the fireplace. "We got her. We got her good!"

"Sheez," I said, as everyone clapped. "You all almost gave me a coronary."

"Now when are ya gonna get it, Marcia." Charlene, Mayfair's only mail carrier, grinned at me. "It's just one word, *y'all*. Not *you all*."

I shrugged, returning her grin. "What can I say? I'm from Maryland. We've only got one foot in the South."

Becky emerged from the crowd of people, smiling, in a white sundress that showed off her tan. I squealed and we gave each other a long, tight hug.

Then I stepped back. "Where's Andy?"

Will appeared at my elbow. "Minding the store in Collinsville."

Someone grabbed my hand and led me through to the kitchen, where my table was covered with an array of casseroles and serving dishes. Sherie Wells handed me a plate and started spooning food onto it.

"Hey, enough." I laughed. "There's only one of me."

Her eyes sparkled. "For now, but you'll be eatin' for two one of these days."

Surprisingly, that statement did not strike fear in my heart as it once would have.

When I'd eaten and exchanged pleasantries with everyone, Will gestured for me to follow him. He led me out the back door, Buddy trailing along. Then he waved his hand to the right.

The sun was beginning to set, casting long shadows in my yard. It took a few seconds for my mind to comprehend what I was looking at.

There were now double wooden gates in my six-foot high privacy fence, about halfway down the side of my yard.

"I hope you don't mind," Will said. "I took the liberty of having Pete add those."

Totally baffled, I turned toward him. "Why?"

He was grinning. "So I can bring my lawn tractor through to mow your side."

I was still confused. "My side of what?"

"Our yard."

"Hunh?"

"Come here." He grabbed my hand and dragged me over to the gates, then unlatched one and threw it open.

Running out onto a neatly cut lawn, where scraggly weeds and palmetto bushes had been a week ago, he yelled back over his shoulder, "Come look."

Buddy thought he was playing and raced after him with a happy woof. Will jumped back and forth, the dog dancing in front of him, until I caught up.

Then Will gestured toward the back of Edna and Dexter's house.

The scent of freshly cut wood filled my nostrils as I looked where he was pointing. A wide, screened-in deck now adorned the back of the dilapidated house.

"The first of many improvements," Will said, pride in his voice, "that I'm going to make to *my* house."

"Your house?"

"Yup. I figured if you need baby steps, then instead of living together, we'll live next door to each other for a while. I bought the place."

"But what about Edna and Dexter? And you can't commute to Collinsville from here."

"They'll stay here until the motel's finished enough for them to live there. And in another month, I'll no longer be working in Collinsville."

"Hunh?" I realized I was sounding like a moron, but Will kept throwing one shocker after another at me.

"You know that election for sheriff they're having in Collins County?"

"Yeah." I was getting a funny feeling about where this was going.

"I'm withdrawing my candidacy." He stuck his thumbs in his belt loops and rocked back on his heels, grinning like a fool. "The good folks will have to choose between Andy or Jamilla."

As the implications sank in, I laughed out loud. Racism is all too often alive and well in rural Florida, and Collins County was about as rural as it gets. But like it or not, the county was about to have its first black sheriff, since both remaining candidates were of African-American persuasion.

"But what are you going to do?" I said.

"I start in six weeks with the Marion County Sheriff's Department, as a detective."

"Wow." I closed the gap between us in two steps, threw my arms around his neck, and gave him a big kiss.

When we broke for air, he said, "Does that mean you're okay with all this?"

"Yes, but you took a big risk. What if I hadn't been?"

He shrugged. "After I got over my disappointment, I'd probably stay in the sheriff's race and come up here to work on my house on my days off. It's a good investment either way. It's structurally sound. Just needs a lot of work."

I stepped back and then twirled around in the middle of the yard. Will's yard. Right next door to mine. Buddy woofed and romped around me.

Suddenly several people's odd behavior made sense. "Pete

was in on this, wasn't he?"

Will nodded. "He brought in a second crew of men who helped me with the deck."

"I can't believe you did all this without me getting a hint of what was going on."

"Well, you have been a bit preoccupied, over there in Buckland Beach," he said, but there was no rancor in his voice. "I also had some help from Mrs. Wells and Edna and Dexter. He cleaned up back here for me." Will waved an arm to encompass the yard. "And the ladies cleaned your house and set up the party."

I grimaced. "Did the police make much of a mess when they searched the house?"

"They didn't go in the house, Pete said. The search warrant was only for the yard. Apparently, the tipster was fairly specific about where the diamonds might be."

I deflated a little. "Tipster as in Larry Merrick. I still can't believe he was behind it all. And that he tried to frame *me*."

Will shrugged. "Sadly, after fifteen years in law enforcement, I can believe it. I've seen too many seemingly law-abiding citizens who turned out to not be." He draped an arm around my shoulders. "But I'm glad it wasn't your friends, the Blacks. They seemed like good people."

"They are." I began steering us back toward the gate, but Will was dragging his feet.

Buddy raced on ahead, back through the gate into my yard.

"Hey," I said, "I forgot to tell you something I learned from the sergeant. Apparently, Merrick was out to get Jake because he took Janey away from him in high school. Janey was Merrick's girl initially. He was planning to marry her."

Will came to a full stop. "And he was holding a grudge all those years?"

"Looks that way."

Larry's tendency to hold a grudge had been his downfall. I'd had trouble figuring out why he'd involved me in that final scene at Rusty's. I wasn't a necessary player. But then it had dawned on me that he was paying me back for rejecting him.

I shook my head. "I was kind of surprised to discover that they're all in their mid-forties. Phelps and Jake look older than that and Larry looks younger."

"Don't know about the sergeant," Will said, "but Jake's lived hard."

"Yes, he has," I agreed. "And Larry probably sold his soul to the devil for perpetual youth," snarky me added. This time I felt no need to rein her in.

"He went to a lot of trouble to set Jake up for the robberies, and for murder."

I turned to face him. "I think greed was his main motivation. Getting back at Jake and Janey was a side benefit. And I don't think murder was his original intention. But once Elsie knew he was involved..." I choked up for a second, flashing back to the feel of that sticky wetness on my hand after cradling her head.

"I wonder how that happened?"

"Knowing Larry as I do, I suspect he felt the need to super-vise..." Too late I realized I'd given away more than I'd intended.

"Knowing him as you do?"

I shrugged, hoping the fading light would cover the heat creeping up my cheeks. "He said something about Rusty saying his name. Elsie must've figured out he was in cahoots with the robbers."

Will chuckled. "In cahoots? Is that another motherism?"

Relieved that I'd distracted him, I tilted my head coquettishly to one side. "No, I think I picked that one up from Edna."

He threw back his head and laughed out loud.

Then I stood on tiptoes and kissed him again.

Just to make sure I had totally gotten his mind off of Larry Merrick.

EPILOGUE

I got a call in late November, on a particularly cool evening for central Florida. It was from Sergeant Phelps.

"Ms. Banks, you're not gonna believe this."

Butterflies fluttered in my stomach as I stared at the flickering flames in my fireplace and wondered what calamity had fouled the case of the Buckland County Sheriff's Department against Larry Merrick.

Buddy stirred at my feet. I scratched under his chin with the toe of my sneaker.

"It looks like you won't have to testify," Phelps said.

"Oh?" Relief attempted to beat back the butterflies, with limited success. I was waiting for the other shoe to drop.

"Merrick finally confessed, in a plea deal. And not just to robbing the pawn shop and Elsie Belenky's murder. There was enough evidence to tie him to the other thefts along the coast as well."

"How'd he pull all that off?"

"Basically the same M.O. in each town. He'd cozy up to the local bikers, preferably the one percenters, until he found one or two who were willing accomplices. And he'd recruit one of the locals to casually case the targets."

"Like the laundromat guy."

"Yeah. He confessed too, by the way. He made it a habit of wandering over to the pawn shop and chatting up Mrs. Belenky about what shipments they had coming in."

My throat tightened at the thought of Elsie Belenky innocently giving up the information that had eventually led to her death.

"I know Merrick was bragging to you about an offshore account," Phelps continued, "but it looks like most of the money was laundered to look like legitimate income–"

"Through his law practice," I guessed.

"Yup. How'd you know?"

"I figured he wasn't all that successful as a lawyer, since he seemed to always have time to help me out."

"Humph," Phelps half snorted. "He was really trying to keep up with whatever you were finding out. His office didn't even have furniture in it, but he was reporting almost two hundred thousand a year, mostly from nonexistent personal injury clients."

I wasn't too surprised. "Thanks for letting me know, Sergeant."

"You're welcome, and say hi to Sheriff Haines for me."

"I'll do that." I disconnected, turned my head and smiled. "Merrick took a plea deal, and Sergeant Phelps says hi."

Said sheriff, whose arm was draped around my shoulders, smiled back.

Except he wasn't a sheriff anymore. He was a detective in the Marion County Sheriff's Department, and my next-door neighbor.

~~~<>~~~

AUTHOR'S NOTES

If you enjoyed this book, please take a moment to leave a short review on the book retailer's site where you downloaded it (and/or other online book retailers). Reviews help with sales, and sales keep the series going! You can find the links for these retailers at the *misterio press* bookstore (http://misteriopress.com/misterio-press-bookstore/#kassandra-lamb).

Also, you may want to go to http://kassandralamb.com to sign up for my newsletter and get updates on new releases, giveaways and sales (and you get a free e-copy of a novella for signing up). I only send out newsletters when I truly have news and you can unsubscribe at any time.

We at *misterio press* pride ourselves on providing our readers with top-quality reads. All of our books are proofread multiple times by several pairs of eyes, but proofreaders are human. If you found errors in this book, please email me at lambkassandra3@gmail.com so the errors can be corrected. Thank you!

Let me spread around some appreciation and then chat a bit about some of the aspects of this story. Then I'll share with you a synopsis of the next story in the series.

A big thank you to my partner in crime at *misterio press*, co-founder Shannon Esposito, whose inital critique of this story had me tearing it apart, adding things, rearranging things, etc. Which is exactly what should happen after a good critique.

Also much gratitude to my wonderful daughter-in-law, romance author, GG Andrew whose eye for detail and feedback regarding all things Millennial are so valuable, to Marilyn Hiliau for her feedback regarding not just the story but also about service dogs and not-for-profit tax issues, and to Vinnie Hansen, my sister author at *misterio*, for her critique and first proofread. And as always, hugs to my wonderful friend, Angi, my other service-dog consultant, and to my patient and long-suffering husband who is my final proofreader.

And I'm dedicating a separate paragraph this time to my brother. He was, as always, my guy and gun consultant, but this time his input was particularly critical since he is a motorcycle enthusiast.

I have tried to be true to everyone's advice. Any errors are strictly mine.

And let me never forget my marvelous editor, Marcy Kennedy, from whom I have learned so much and who still catches many details, big and small, that make my stories so much better.

One of my goals with this story was to debunk some of the myths and misconceptions about motorcyclists (or bikers, as they prefer to be called). But the idea of distinctive-looking motorcycles being the main evidence against alleged robbers also intrigued me as a story concept.

The Indian Motorcycle Company, founded in 1901, built the first motorcycles in the U.S., but they stopped making the bikes in 1953. The rights to the Indian name were bought and sold several times by various companies, and production of the bikes finally resumed in 1998. Today, Polaris Industries manufactures Indian bikes.

These motorcycles have very distinctive curved fenders with long skirts that come down on the sides. All the various owners and manufacturers have stayed true to this unique design.

Another goal of this book, as it is in each of the stories in this series, was to illustrate some of the challenges our combat veterans face when they return to civilian life, especially if they have suffered "invisible" injuries such as PTSD and traumatic brain injury. The aftereffects of TBI—memory loss, balance issues, anger management problems, etc.—can take years to dissipate and some sufferers have residual symptoms even after that. These issues complicate their lives, especially when those around them fail to realize the extent of their impact or how long recovery can take.

And last but not least, I like to highlight the things that service dogs do for our veterans and how they are trained to do these tasks. I couldn't do much with the training angle in this story, since Marcia is "between dogs" but I was glad for the opportunity to showcase how the dogs can apply deep pressure therapy to help with anxiety.

Deep pressure (sometimes called compression therapy) has been used for quite some time with children on the autism spectrum to calm their overactive nervous systems. In more recent times, it has been used for anxiety disorders and PTSD.

I don't think the verdict is in research-wise on *how* deep pressure works but it does seem to activate the calming mechanisms of the human nervous system, causing a slowing of the heart rate and lessening of the subjective experience of anxiety.

As I've mentioned before, the towns of Mayfair and Collinsville and Collins County are fictitious locations. For this book, I invented yet another fictitious town and county in Florida, Buckland Beach and Buckland County. Daytona Beach, Ormond Beach and Ormond-By-The-Sea are real places, as are Flagler Beach and Crescent Beach. And certainly there are real hospitals and Honda dealerships in Daytona Beach, but the ones in this story, Daytona General Hospital and Daytona Honda, are figments of my imagination.

However, Publix grocery stores are very real and are scattered all over Florida. In my opinion, it is one of the best grocery store chains in the country. They pride themselves on friendly service and they hire disabled workers as often as possible. There are no doubt several dozen real counterparts to my fictitious bagger, Derek.

I'm currently outlining Book 4, *Patches in the Rye*. Let me take a moment to clarify about the titles in this series. They only loosely relate to the events in the stories, since I have no desire to rewrite the classics whose titles I am mimicking (or some might say, hijacking).

Here's a brief synopsis of *Patches in the Rye, A Marcia Banks and Buddy Mystery*, Book 4:

Service dog trainer, Marcia Banks is almost knocked on her keister as she rings the doorbell of a new client. Instead of being greeted by the wheelchair-bound former Navy seaman she's expecting, the door is ripped open by a young woman who whips past her in tears. Inside, the client, Roger Campbell is fuming, and consumed with worry for his younger sister, who's dating a man with an extensive history of delinquency.

Roger has heard rumors that Marcia possesses some investigative skills and he wants to hire her to check out his sister's boyfriend. At first she resists the idea, but money is tight, as usual, so she agrees to see what she can do.

With the help of her mentor dog Buddy, Marcia attempts to juggle the training of Patches, a mutt so ugly he's cute, with the investigating. But she soon discovers the situation is more complicated than the client had assumed.

The young man's misdeeds seem to be in the past as he claims, but someone doesn't want them to stay there. And a long-buried secret threatens to destroy the very family Marcia and Buddy are trying to help.

ABOUT THE AUTHOR

Kassandra Lamb has never been able to decide which she loves more, psychology or writing. In college, she realized that writers need a day job in order to eat, so she studied psychology. After a career as a psychotherapist and college professor, she is now retired and can pursue her passion for writing. She spends most of her time in an alternate universe with her characters. The portal to this universe, aka her computer, is located in Florida, where her husband and dog catch occasional glimpses of her. She and her husband spend part of each summer in her native Maryland, where her Kate Huntington series is based.

Kass is currently working on Book 10 of the Kate Huntington mystery series and Book 4 of the Marcia Banks and Buddy cozy mysteries. She also has four novellas out in the Kate on Vacation series (lighter reads along the lines of cozy mysteries but with the same main characters as the Kate Huntington series).

To read and see more about Kassandra and her characters you can go to http://kassandralamb.com. Be sure to sign up for the newsletter there to get a heads up about new releases, plus special offers and bonuses for subscribers. (New subscribers get a free e-copy of the first Kate on Vacation novella.)

Kass's e-mail is lambkassandra3@gmail.com and she loves hearing from readers! She's also on Facebook (https://www.facebook.com/kassandralambauthor) and hangs out some on Twitter @KassandraLamb. She blogs about psychological topics and other random things at http://misteriopress.com.

Turn the page for other great series from *misterio press*.